ADAM

A companion novel to the
Perfect World Series

SHARI SAKURAI

Published in the United Kingdom by Farnhurst Publishing

1

ISBN: 978-0-9928024-7-9

www.sharisakurai.com

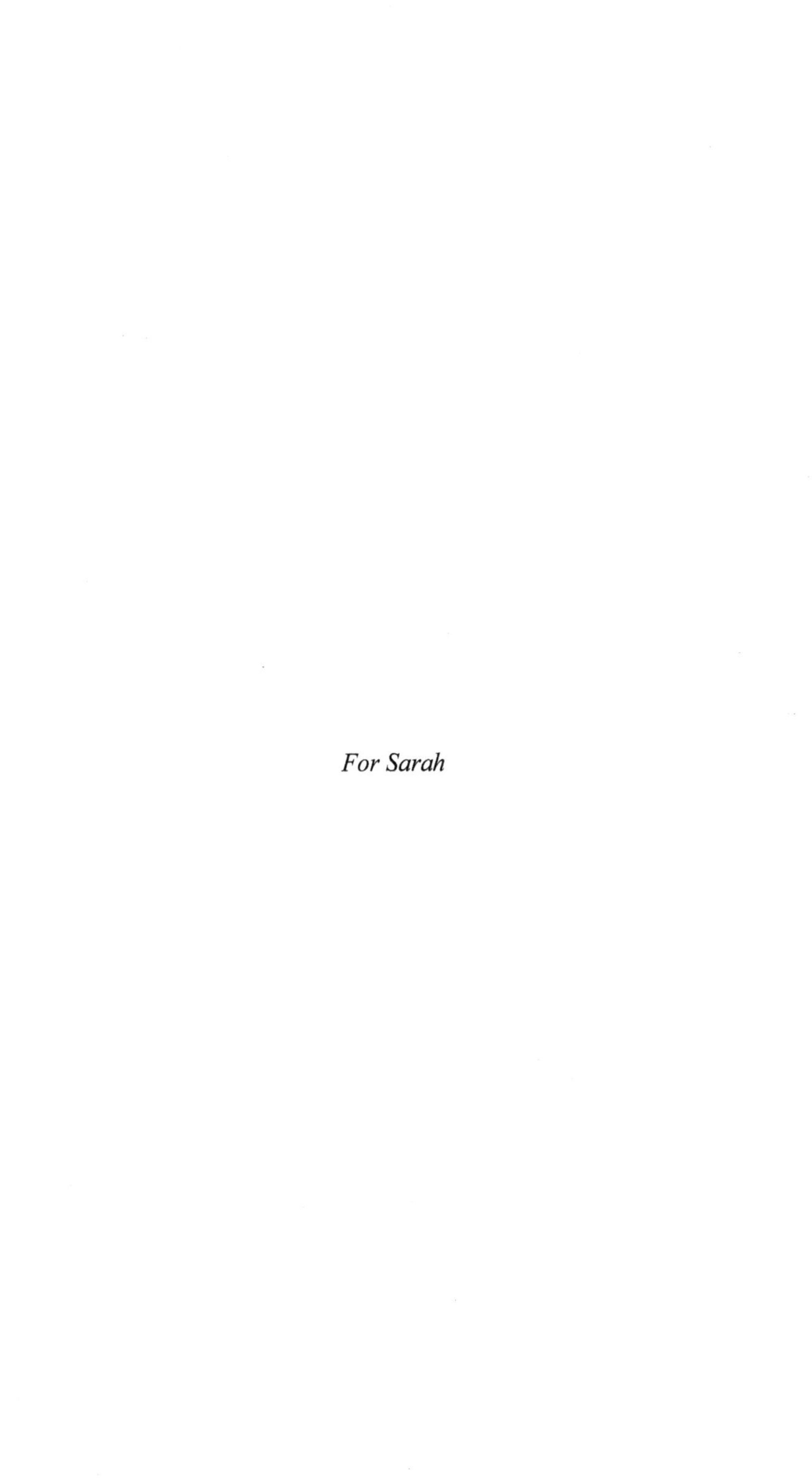

For Sarah

ACKNOWLEDGMENTS

Thank you very much to Mum, Dad and Sarah for all their help with this companion novel.

PROLOGUE

Adam Larimore stood on the balcony in silence. So many thoughts were going round and round in his head. The most prominent was that he hadn't meant for things to turn out the way that they had. Revenge was all he had cared about and had influenced his every action. For three years there had been no room in his life for anything else. Now things were changing and Adam wasn't sure that he wanted them to. The prospect was terrifying and it was far easier to continue down the path that he was already walking, even if it wasn't what he truly wanted anymore.

"I know what it's like to think that you don't have a choice," Eric finally broke the silence. His expression appeared pained as he spoke, "But you do now. You can let things continue as they are or you can turn things around."

It was naïve of him to think that Adam had any kind of choice. Adam was a criminal. He was wanted for murder, terrorism offences and so many other charges that he could no longer recall. There was no way back from this. Even in the beginning his choices had been limited. Now they were non-existent. The only option open to Adam was to keep going.

"What if I want to continue?" Adam questioned with some vague curiosity as he mulled over Eric's words. He was certain that the bitterness in his tone was not lost on the other man. "What will you do?"

How could Eric liken it to his situation? Eric's actions had always been for good. Adam's had been motivated by anger and a desire for revenge.

Six months ago, using his computer expertise and knowledge of the Government systems to his advantage, Adam had hacked into the program that controlled the defence shields encircling the north of the city. The shields had been developed to protect London from foreign missile strikes and other outside threats. Once he had cut off north London, Adam had established his headquarters in the Serpentines – a luxury apartment block that had been originally built for Government officials – and set in motion his plan for revenge. His plan had involved the L.S.A's special agent Eric Rawlins. Eric had been genetically engineered to become the country's 'superhero' and defend London against acts of terrorism. However, Eric had been lied to all of his life and his popularity had been used to manipulate the public into favouring the L.S.A. Adam had shown Eric the truth just over a week ago and they had become lovers. At first this was only so that Adam could manipulate Eric to his advantage. Yet quickly this, and Adam's feelings, had changed.

"I don't think you do."

Eric's response struck a chord inside of Adam and it was almost unbearable. Adam couldn't even bring himself to look at his lover. Instead he reached into his jacket pocket and took out the small metal box that he kept his cigarettes and lighter in. Adam didn't particularly want a cigarette, but he did want a distraction.

"I didn't know you smoked," Eric commented softly.

There's so much you still don't know about me...

"Only occasionally. Do you want one?" Adam said out loud as he offered the packet to him. Naturally Eric declined.

"Last night," he continued cautiously, "you said that you continued because carrying on was easier than facing what you'd done. I can understand your feelings but you can't keep on doing all this. You have to face it eventually and it'll be worse for you the longer you avoid it."

Please don't push this...

"And what would you have me do?" Adam demanded. He didn't want to feel so conflicted and a part of him was annoyed with Eric for making him feel this way. Things were so much simpler before he started this. "Give myself up? Ivan will have me killed if I do that."

Eric appeared distressed by Adam's words. He took a moment before replying. "You've shown me that the L.S.A and Government are corrupt. That the country has been manipulated ever since the end of the war. We need to tell everyone the truth. That's how you can make amends."

Eric's naivety and belief in their country was laughable. Adam had long since abandoned any faith he might have had. "At the moment you are London's beloved superhero," he pointed out quietly. "The minute the country finds out that you're working with me you'll be discredited. No one will believe you. The L.S.A will issue a warrant for your arrest and they'll have the country's support."

"I still want to help you," Eric insisted with some

desperation edging into his voice.

"You can't. It doesn't matter what I do," Adam stated matter-of-factly in response to this. He was aware that he appeared cold and unfeeling, but this was an automatic defence mechanism that he had built up within the last couple of years which prevented him from reacting any differently.

Carrying on became easier than facing what I had done

His breakdown last night had been partly orchestrated to further manipulate Eric's feelings for him, although more and more Adam was realising that he wasn't faking it. He really did care for the hero, and this realisation was terrifying.

He couldn't stay out here any longer. The situation was making Adam uncomfortable. He had to refocus he told himself in annoyance as he put out his cigarette and turned to go back inside his penthouse.

"Adam, I love you," Eric stated tenderly as he reached out and took hold of Adam's wrist.

Adam had known that this was coming. Eric had a dangerous tendency to wear his heart on his sleeve. It was how Adam had been able to manipulate him up until now.

"No you don't," he replied firmly as he freed himself from Eric's grasp. They both knew that Eric was being sincere; Adam just didn't want those words to be true.

Because I love you too

"I do," Eric said softly as he took Adam's hand again. The younger man didn't respond to the kiss that followed or when Eric wrapped his arms around him and pulled Adam against his chest. Adam felt regret welling up inside of him. He wanted so desperately to suggest that they leave. That they take Perses and fly away from everything. But Adam couldn't do that. As much as he loved Eric he couldn't turn back now.

He had to finish what he had started.

"You can't say that to me," he said finally as he pulled himself free of Eric's embrace. With no further words he hurried back inside. Much to his dismay Eric followed him.

"Adam—"

Against his better judgement Adam allowed Eric to momentarily catch up. However, the hero found himself somewhat at a loss for words.

"I…" The look he gave Adam was so pained that the younger man couldn't stand it.

"I need some time to myself," Adam stated without giving Eric a chance to consider his response. He practically ran through to his bedroom and shut the door behind him. Adam slumped down onto the bed and buried his head in his hands. He had to get a hold of himself. This was the path he had chosen. There was no turning back now even if he wanted there to be.

"Don't come in here," he warned when heard Eric approaching the door.

"Adam, we need to talk. I don't understand why I've upset—"

"Go away," Adam snapped sharply, cutting Eric off before he could say anything further.

"Adam—"

"I want to be alone, Eric."

"Fine, I'll be out here if you decide you actually care enough to talk about this."

Adam sighed softly, but he didn't reply. He didn't want to talk. Eric admitting his feelings had made Adam even more conflicted. However, one thing Adam did know was that he couldn't give up his revenge. The desire to make Ivan pay had kept him strong since his stepfamily died. It was all that Adam had cared about for so long now.

CHAPTER ONE

Saturday 5th March 2112, Sector Four, Old Greenwich, North London

Adam Larimore sighed to himself as he slumped down onto the metal chair. The overseeing officer took the seat on the other side of the table. It was just after 7am and Adam had been arrested in Sector Four, Old Greenwich the night before.

The Government police station was a small temporary building consisting only of a ground floor which was constructed of steel with a large glass window in the front. The doors were all operated electronically with thumbprint recognition. There was the main reception, a holding cell and an interview room. The interview room was small and barely had room for the table and chairs. It was drab and the walls showed the exposed metal panelling. The floor was tiled. This combination of materials lowered the temperature in the building considerably. The station itself was only designed to hold people accused of minor crimes or until they were handed over to the main station in Sector One.

Adam wasn't quite sure how much he'd had to drink last night, however, the pounding headache that he had been left with this morning was a good indication that it had been a lot.

"Please state your full name and age," the officer opposite him requested as he took out his portable touch-screen computer. The Government police dealt with most national crime within the cities whilst international, security threats and Government-interests related crimes were dealt with directly by the London Security Agency.

In 2049 a series of Great Tsunamis had devastated much of the world. These tsunamis had formed as a result of massive undersea earthquakes. On that fateful day in August life had changed forever. Chaos and war followed as the remaining countries became desperate and turned on each other. Surviving Government officials in England had formed the London Security Agency – L.S.A – and it was the L.S.A's job to protect London from hostile nations as well as fractious groups within the country. The new Government had been in power since 2049 and had poured all of its resources into technology that it believed could prevent future disasters and move England forward in its recovery. At first technology was salvaged from the ruins and survivors repaired what they could until the water had receded enough to restore a working Government in London. Once the new political power had been established and the country brought back to order they could begin to rebuild.

The defence shields around London and other main cities were the first major advance. At the time funding had been limited and the Government had been forced to prioritise this over helping civilians still in dire situations after the disasters.

The rationale that there wouldn't be a country to rebuild if England didn't exit the war was widely accepted and thus there was little opposition to this decision.

The dome-shaped shields with inbuilt sensors detected any unauthorised access by land, sea or air. Laser gunfire obliterated any hostile craft that came within the shields' range. With this technology England was able to isolate itself from the war and watch as the fighting nations destroyed each other.

After the war came the era known as the age of technology and genetic engineering. With a much depleted population the Government turned to science once more for help. For the first five years the focus was on rebuilding and gradually jobs were created and currency was re-introduced. Individuals with a talent for creating computer programs or who had a scientific or medial background prospered whilst the majority of the population remained in poverty. The Government did little to close the class gap; it was to be expected and their focus had to be on recovery and growth.

Natural conception was made illegal, and unauthorised pregnancies were terminated. All prospective parents had to be approved in L.S.A-run facilities. Approved parents were asked to attend a consultation at the London Hospital of Advanced Genetic Sciences (L.H.A.G.S) where they could select their baby's gender, hair colour and eye colour. This selection ensured the best possible gene pool and that the babies carried no genetic defects or diseases. To make sure that the population grew at a steady rate that the Government could support couples were only allowed one child. More affluent parents could also opt to pay for other desired traits.

Adam was one such child. His father was Victor Larimore,

the chairman and owner of Larimore Systems. Larimore Systems revolutionised computers and weapons technology in 2071 when it was formed and was the main supplier to the Government and L.S.A. The company and his genius had made Victor billions. Yet he had no one to inherit his fortune.

Victor had paid fifty million pounds for the perfect heir to his empire. At the time of Adam's creation he had no wife and he was getting old enough to consider the possibility that he might never meet someone. Annaliese Merrik was a surrogate and she had not wished to have any contact with her son after his birth.

Adam had discovered the truth when he was twelve years old. After asking so many times about his mother, Adam had hacked into his father's computer system and found the files detailing his creation and birth. What he had discovered was that he was a living job description. Every character trait and every gift had been carefully selected to produce the ideal successor to Victor Larimore. Adam's IQ was of genius level. In fact he had never met anyone who could match it. He couldn't get sick or contract diseases. He could also heal when injured and would age more slowly than normal people. He had to drink almost twice what it would take to get a normal person drunk before he would get a hangover the following day. Immortality, even with so many scientific advances, was still an impossible dream, but Adam came pretty close to it. Adam was often told that many would do anything for his 'gifts' yet he couldn't bring himself to be thankful for them. He didn't feel real. He felt like one of his father's investments. And worse still a disappointment.

"Please state your full name and age," the police officer repeated irately when he realised that he didn't have Adam's attention. The younger man glared disdainfully at him. As if he didn't know who Adam was!

The officer wore the standard uniform, consisting of a white shirt with a bullet and knife-proof dark blue vest, dark blue trousers and black shoes. The words 'Government Police' were stitched onto the front of the vest.

He was probably only a few years older than himself, Adam thought. He was solidly built with broad shoulders and with his sleeves rolled up Adam could see, and appreciate, his muscular arms. Dark brown hair with a sprinkling of light highlights was cut to just below the tops of his ears. Hazel eyes regarded Adam with indifference. For now.

Adam deliberately held the officer's gaze as he slouched down further on the metal-framed chair. Slowly he lifted his right leg up and slammed a boot-clad foot down on the metal surface of the table separating them. He repeated the action with this left leg crossing them at the ankles. A smirk curved his lips as this provoked an irate response from the other man.

"Take your feet off of the table and state your full name and age please."

Adam ignored him.

"Take your feet off of the table. *Now*," the officer repeated, his tone of voice taking a harder edge as he fidgeted in his own seat.

"Make me…" Adam's gaze flitted to his LCD I.D badge pinned to his vest. "Joel," he added with a grin.

Officer Joel Banks scowled and shook his head although it was clear from his hesitant stance that he had no intention of making Adam do anything. Most policemen were afraid of Adam's father, and with good reason. Victor had more than enough influence to ensure that the man was stripped of his rank and never worked in the force again.

"Any chance you could get me a glass of water? And possibly something for my headache?"

"You think you're untouchable don't you?" Banks retorted angrily. "Sitting there so fucking smug and ordering me about."

"I *am* untouchable. But that isn't my fault."

"Yeah well we'll see," he turned his attention back to his computer. "The suspect is refusing to cooperate so I, Officer Joel Banks, will confirm identity on his behalf. The date is Saturday 5th March 2112 and the suspect is eighteen year old Adam Victor James Larimore of Venewood, Ward Two – Old Camden, Sector One. Fingerprint analysis will confirm my verbal identification."

Banks pressed part of the screen and got up. Larimore Systems had transformed portable computers. The slim-line silver or grey computers with the immensely popular Eos System that had been developed by Larimore Systems were now commonplace and used by the Government, Government services and L.S.A as well as individuals.

Banks brought the computer round to Adam's side of the table and held it out in front of him. "Press your forefinger in the centre of the blue square."

Adam did as he was told, although the handcuffs on his wrists hindered his movement somewhat.

"Happy now?" he asked when the officer withdrew the screen.

Banks scowled and sat back down.

"I don't suppose I could have that glass of water?"

"Shut up."

"Or what?" Adam dared. He caught the officer's eye and

grinned. Thanks to his slim build, pale complexion, long silky black hair and deep midnight blue eyes Adam was well aware that his androgynous appearance was confusing to many men and he often used this to wrong-foot the rookie officers that arrested him. He just liked messing with them and none of them dared say anything to their superior officers or to Adam's father. He shifted his position slightly and gave Banks another suggestive stare. The other man was definitely uncomfortable now and this heightened Adam's amusement.

"You know I'll be out of here by eight."

"You think so?" Banks questioned irritably.

"I know so. Feel free to look me up if you like."

Banks laughed shortly and shook his head. "Shut up."

Slowly and deliberately Adam uncrossed his legs. This action caused the leather trousers he was wearing to squeak. Regular clothing that was produced was so bland and boring so all of his clothes were custom made and very expensive. He noted a slight tear in one knee as he moved and sighed. It must have been damaged when the arresting officer had shoved him to the ground.

"You look like you need a good time. I can give you one if you like, *Joel*."

"Please remain quiet unless you want to get yourself into even more trouble," Banks warned him in annoyance.

"There's no need to be embarrassed," Adam drawled as he leaned back further in his chair. "You're not the first man to look at me that way."

"You really are something else aren't you," Banks snapped, shaking his head in utter disgust. "Now I suggest you stop this before you make things even worse for yourself."

Adam shrugged. "Your loss."

“I very much doubt it.”

Adam sniggered and was preparing a retort when the metal door slid open. Two older men entered. The first was Ivan Williams; the Chief of Police. His background was working as a general in the military until an injury to his spine had forced him to retire. Whilst he had made more or less a full recovery he was limited on what he could do in the field and so took the position offered to him by the Government. Ivan was also Adam’s godfather. He stood tall at six foot; the rectangular shape of his face and set of his jaw made his appearance harsh and unapproachable. His black hair had started to turn grey in places in recent years. However, despite his stern appearance, he was the more reasonable and fair of the two men who entered the room.

The second man was Adam’s father.

Victor Larimore was a head shorter than Ivan’s six foot yet somehow he appeared more imposing. He always wore business suits, which like Adam’s own clothing, had been custom ordered and made. His hair had once been as dark as Adam’s own but there was now more silver in it than there had been in recent years. Victor’s eyes were dark brown and unfeeling. There seemed to be more lines on his face nowadays and a tiredness about him that hadn’t been there previously. This made his mood even more disagreeable.

“Get your feet off the table right now!” he barked furiously at his son. Adam’s smirk faded as he did as he was told. Without another word his father approached. Adam tensed; he knew what was coming.

The blow startled even Banks, but Adam didn’t get to see much of his reaction as the power behind it almost toppled him from the chair. He raised his cuffed hands and touched his split lower lip, wincing at the secondary discomfort that his contact brought about.

"Victor," Ivan warned when it looked as though Adam's father wanted to strike him again. Adam raised his head as his father sat down on the empty chair beside him.

Ivan said something inaudible to Banks and the younger officer left the room. His godfather seemed equally displeased as he took the seat that Banks had vacated.

"Has Officer Banks detailed the charges against you?" Ivan asked as he consulted the computer.

"No, we were still getting...erm…acquainted," Adam answered with a small forced smile that caused his mouth to smart painfully. He grimaced and his amusement faded.

"You are charged with vandalising Government property and assaulting the police officer who attempted to apprehend you. Do you understand these charges?"

"Ivan, surely we can skip all this?" Victor interjected. "I'll pay the fine and any associated damages."

Ivan frowned unhappily. "I'm afraid it isn't that simple, Victor. Didn't anyone tell you exactly what happened?"

"He hit a policeman. I know it's not good, but—"

"With a glass bottle!" Adam cut in with frustration. It looked as though his father was merely going to throw money at this to make it go away. *Again.*

"Officer Reynolds is in a bad way. He could lose his sight in his right eye," Ivan said evenly. "As you can imagine I am under pressure to ensure that his attacker does not go unpunished."

"Look," Victor stated, "I can guarantee that all medical care will be paid for and that the compensation will be substantial. All I ask is that Adam is spared a prison sentence."

Adam sighed and tuned them out. They were behaving as though he wasn't in the room as usual. Whilst he did feel regret and guilt at hurting the officer, his overwhelming frustration and anger towards his father left little room for other emotions. He just wanted to lash out, to hurt the man and make him feel even a tenth of what Adam was feeling. Nothing he did gained the reaction that he wanted. All it did was make his father hate him more.

Finally, after ten minutes and the agreement of a very sizable amount in compensation, Ivan decided that he could pull some strings and have Adam released after all.

"Victor," Ivan said somewhat hesitantly as he freed Adam from the handcuffs. "This is the third offence in two months. Perhaps you ought to consider getting Adam some professional help. I have access to the best doctors in the country. Why don't you let me make a couple of calls?"

"There's no need for any of that, thank you," Victor answered curtly.

"What do you think, Adam?" Ivan turned to his godson, much to his father's chagrin.

Adam shook his head, "Same time next week, Ivan?"

"For your sake I hope not," Ivan murmured in defeat. "I have arranged for some private transport to take you both home."

Ivan escorted them through the reception in silence. As they walked by the desk Adam caught Officer Banks' eye. He gave him a smirk, which was met with a look of anger.

"Seven-forty," Adam called over his shoulder. The officer beside Officer Banks placed a restraining hand on his arm when it looked as though Banks wanted to respond, and murmured something inaudible.

A private tram stood outside the station. The driver regarded Adam with disgust; a look that he was used to by now. He got in and slumped down on a seat at the back. Electric trams were affordable public transport and also energy efficient. Each tram had a first class section for those who could afford to pay the premium. This section had comfortable leather padded seating, tables and even a drinks dispenser. Inbuilt into the rear of each chair was a basic Information Bank screen that displayed information about the tram system and any news that might impact on the journey. Adam didn't care for the comforts of first class and usually when he travelled he sat with everyone else. It represented a lot of what was wrong with their new and perfect world. Society seemed to have taken a step back rather than forward. Only the superrich had any real power.

Throughout the journey his father remained silent. He did not speak to his son again until they arrived home.

Venewood had been the Larimore family home since before Adam was born. The style of home, he believed, had been referred to as mock Tudor back in the early part of the last century. It had been modelled on the home that his father's parents had owned before the Great Tsunamis. Adam had only ever seen one photograph of the old Venewood estate, and he had to admit that his father had recreated an almost exact likeness. To do this Victor had purchased a sizeable plot of land in Old Camden. The land used to have several old disused shops upon it, which were then demolished. For private individuals gaining planning permission from the Government was impossible without a vast amount of money and Victor Larimore certainly had that.

From the outside the five bedroom home was a proud

tribute to the old Venewood estate. It was half-timbered with real wooden beams to the upper storey. The bricks forming the lower storey had been sourced from outside of the city. Incorporated into the external structure was the modern electronic thumbprint operated front door and state-of-the-art security system. Victor had spent millions on the unique home. Adam doubted that there were more than a handful of real, lived in houses in the country.

Adam trailed behind his father as they approached Venewood. He could tell by the stance of the man that he was barely keeping his temper in check. When they reached the door Victor unlocked it and stepped inside.

The hallway was open plan and directly in the centre of the vast room was a hand-carved wooden staircase leading up to the first floor. Modern metal doors that were painted in dark brown to try to match the traditional staircasing led off to various bedrooms. Downstairs there was an ultra-modern kitchen furnished in metal, a living room, a second reception room and a formal dining room. There was a gymnasium in the basement.

As Adam had anticipated Victor stuck him again. He grunted in pain as the blow knocked him to the marble floor. Adam lay there and tensed, expecting a further assault. However, this time it was not forthcoming.

"Get up!" his father demanded furiously. Tentatively Adam did as he was told. His head was ringing with pain and he felt a little dizzy as he climbed to his feet.

"Half a million pounds. That is how much you have cost me today, not to mention the effect that it might have on the company. What the hell did you think you were doing, Adam? You're very lucky that Ivan is such a good friend to us.

Otherwise you would be facing a very lengthy prison sentence."

"What does it matter?" Adam retorted bitterly. "I could serve fifteen years and still come out appearing as though I am in my twenties!"

"You're such an ungrateful boy. So many would give anything to have been born with your gifts."

"*Born*?" Adam echoed with a scornful laugh. "I was *made*. I was *created* to inherit your precious empire. You never wanted me. I'm just another investment to you, aren't I?"

"A poor investment," Victor returned angrily.

Adam shook his head as he tried not to show just how much those words had stung.

"You know if you've quite finished I'd like to take a painkiller and sleep off my hangover."

"No I am not *quite finished.* As chairman of Larimore Systems I am suspending you for a month without pay for your unacceptable behaviour. And as your father I am revoking all security clearance needed for you to leave this house. That revoke includes computer access. You need to stop all this now, Adam."

"You really don't have a fucking clue do you?"

"You will not speak to me like that. I have given you everything and you only throw it back in my face. I am your father and you will—"

"My father?" Adam cut in furiously as a lump started to form in his throat. What did he have to do? How far did he have to go to get through to the man? "When have you ever been a father to me?"

This gained a reaction, but only one of more anger. "How dare you—"

"Victor! Adam!" A third voice cut him off. Adam glanced in the direction of the stairs and saw Eleanor Larimore quickly descending them. She was wearing a pink silk robe and her pale, thin face was free from makeup. Her long blonde hair was in a tussled cloud from sleep.

Eleanor was Adam's stepmother and their mutual dislike was barely hidden when no one was around. In front of Adam's father, however, she pretended to make attempts at getting along with him.

Eleanor was forty-six years old. She was the daughter of a judge and even though it could be argued that she didn't need the money, Adam was of the opinion that Eleanor had married his father for his fortune. Despite his anger at Victor, Adam hated the idea that Eleanor was deceiving him.

She reached the bottom of the stairs and went over to her husband.

"Victor," she gently placed a hand on his arm. "Remember what the doctor said about your blood pressure?"

"We've just come from the police station *again*, Ellie."

She sighed softly and leaned up to press a brief kiss to his lips before turning to Adam.

"Why don't you go upstairs, Adam?" she suggested sweetly as though he were still a child. Adam gave her a disgusted look, however, he was quite keen to leave his father's company and so did as he was asked.

Tears of frustration were falling by the time he made it to the sanctuary of his bedroom. Adam slumped face down onto his bed, a sob muffled by the pillows. He almost couldn't take this anymore. He hadn't wanted to hurt anyone. He just didn't know how to deal with, or rid himself of, the constant anger burning inside of him. Drinking numbed some of his emotions although all it seemed to do was turn him into someone else entirely. Someone who was out of control and cared little for property or people. Adam didn't want to be that person, but he didn't know who he was either. How could he? He had been created as Victor Larimore's heir and nothing more. Every part of him had been specified as though he were a job description and not a person. He wasn't even wanted. Not really. His father was too obsessed over adding to his billions to even notice Adam half of the time. Their housekeeper had practically raised him.

April Turrell had been the Larimore's housekeeper for twenty years and had been the closest thing to a mother that Adam had. April had died four years ago. It had been cancer. Adam had watched her succumb within months. All the technology and genetic advances and still there was no cure for that terrible disease. It was nature's selection process, Victor had explained to his grieving son. Even if humanity did find a cure eventually an even worse illness would arise to take cancer's place. There were some things that were even beyond the control of science.

After that Adam had felt even more alone. Soon misery had turned into anger and he could barely remember a time before. He just wanted his father to acknowledge him and at the same time he wanted to hurt the man. Ruining the Larimore name was a good way to do this and it provided an outlet for Adam's rage.

Officer Reynolds is in a bad way. He could lose his sight in his right eye

He flinched as he recalled the policeman's scream and the sight of blood running down his cheek. He hadn't deserved that and Adam didn't even know why he did it. Being drunk was just an excuse. So what did that say about him? *I don't want to be that person...* Adam drew a sharp breath and pressed his face into the pillow once more. After a few minutes he heard his father and Eleanor making their way back up the stairs. Neither came in to see him.

CHAPTER TWO

Adam smirked to himself as he watched the live stream security footage of his father and Eleanor leaving Venewood for the night. The rest of the weekend had dragged with agonising slowness. With little to do here, especially without computer access, Adam had spent the time alone. This had given him too much time to think about things. Even a few days later his actions shocked him. He had been in trouble before, but he'd never actually hurt someone seriously. Adam had tentatively asked his father if he had heard how the officer was. Victor had said that he would check with Ivan tonight. Whether he would or not Adam didn't know. His father had appeared surprised that Adam would ask. *Does he really think I'm such a monster that I wouldn't care?* Adam had asked himself. His thoughts had not lingered on this. He hadn't been certain that he was ready for the answer.

Today was Adam's nineteenth birthday; an event that did not usually go unmarked. This year, however, his father had thought that an additional suitable punishment would be to cancel any plans to celebrate and leave Adam in the house alone whilst he and his wife went to dinner at the Williams' apartment. Joseph, Adam's stepbrother, was seeing his girlfriend and so Adam had the house to himself. Not that he planned on staying in either.

It had taken him only half an hour to circumvent the block that his father had put on his computer access. Ten minutes later and Adam had also dealt with the security program that had prevented him from leaving the house. Re-adding his thumbprint to the clearance protocols had been easy once he had got into the system and he wondered if his father had actually thought that any security program could keep Adam a prisoner.

Adam sat down at his desk as he logged into his bank account. The usual gift of five thousand pounds had been deposited. It was less than Joseph had received two months earlier. Adam's stepbrother had also been given a car. Private transport for individuals had been outlawed over fifty years ago due to the high pollution levels of before the Great Tsunamis, however, Victor had got around this by claiming that the car was required for Larimore Systems' Government contracts. Adam had not been surprised that the application for ownership had been approved given as Victor Larimore's social circle included both the Prime Minister and the Chief of Police.

Adam had known better than to expect such an extravagant gift on his birthday. He scowled at the media capsule containing the holographic birthday card and message from his father and Eleanor. Adam knew the spiel by now and had not bothered to watch it yet. His father would wish him well and say how proud he was of him. This was all a lie. Victor couldn't care less about his son. And yet Adam so desperately wanted to be proved wrong.

Firmly he crushed these thoughts. He transferred one thousand pounds onto his payment card. Payment cards were increasingly popular and the Government encouraged their use as they helped to combat counterfeit money which had increased in production in recent years within the poorer areas of the city. The card resembled the credit cards of the last century and was made of thin aluminium. It had a chip inside which computers could read and that could also be scanned to put credit on.

Adam's bedroom, like the rest of the house, was fitted out with modern and state-of-the-art furnishings. His silver-framed double bed stood in the middle of the room underneath an electronically operated window. The bedroom walls were white with a silver border running at high-level just underneath the ceiling. His wardrobe doors were also electronically operated and the wardrobe was built into the room. Aside from the desk and two bedside cabinets there was little in the way of other furnishings or personal belongings. Adam didn't care much for material objects aside from his custom outfits and his computers. This was ironic seeing as he was one of the few individuals in the city with enough money to buy trivial items.

Material consumerism wasn't encouraged at any rate. The Government insisted that all production of goods was strictly regulated in order to protect resources. Yet these restrictions did not apply to technology that benefitted them and the security of the nation. Public Information Banks were common place on the streets and were free to access. There were low-cost portable computers available and Adam knew, thanks to Larimore Systems' Government contracts, that this was simply so that they could keep control. Therefore all Prime Ministers always ensured that there was money available for technology and scientific advances. This was also how the Government made the majority of its money. Mainly through taxes associated with the technology or by sales of Government-produced software, games, music, films and other programs that could be bought and downloaded relatively cheaply. It all added up and Adam suspected that the Government made a lot more money from technology than they alluded to.

Adam switched off his computer before making his way over to his wardrobe. He already knew what he was going to wear tonight. Clothing for the general population was produced in warehouses around the country on city outskirts. They produced all the same kind of plain clothing with little originality. They were cheaply made and affordable to those struggling on the smallest wages. The rich, however, could order custom clothing in more luxurious fabrics and designs. They were created in the same warehouses. The men and women making them probably only saw a fraction of what was paid for them as most of the money went towards materials, and the profit to the company that ran the warehouse.

Cotton was in limited supply so most clothing was produced from polyester, which was manufactured in cities north of the country. Like with most industries, there was a limit on production and kiosks were only allowed to reorder once most of their stock had been sold.

Adam quickly got changed into his chosen outfit. He had ordered the long-sleeve black top a month ago especially for tonight. It was what had been referred to in the last century as a 'distressed' look with deliberate tears and shreds of fabric hanging off of it. There was a large section of the fabric cut away completely from the middle of the garment, beginning just above his navel and travelling downwards. This had been replaced with black netting that had also been popular over a hundred years ago. Adam had taken a great deal of time to research twentieth and twenty-first century fashions. To begin with he had dressed in this way purely to annoy his father. Now Adam genuinely liked his unique style.

With his new top he chose to wear a pair of close fitting denim black jeans. He carefully ran a brush through his long hair, applied his dramatic eyeliner and pulled on his favourite black jacket before leaving his bedroom.

Adam had deliberately left the surveillance camera filming and he waved at the silver sphere mounted next to the front door as he left Venewood. He was certainly going to be caught and Adam cared little for this.

The tram stop was just down the street from Venewood and there were a few people waiting when he arrived. One older woman gave him a withering stare. Evidently his behaviour last Saturday night had been reported in the Information Bank. The Information Bank was Government-controlled news and information that was released to the general population via the Internet. It was all screened and was careful not to depict them or the L.S.A in a negative way. Ivan would have done his best to get the news of Adam's latest arrest omitted, but it seemed as though he had not been successful.

Adam only had to wait a couple of minutes before the tram pulled up. The tram was equipped with the latest computer technology and Adam pressed his payment card against the reader as he embarked. The fare would be debited when he scanned his card again prior to disembarking.

Adam sat down next to one of the windows. His destination in old Tower Hamlets would take about forty minutes to reach. Old Tower Hamlets ward had been one of the areas worst hit by the Great Tsunamis. In the aftermath available resources had gone into re-establishing a Government and setting up relief aid in the areas that were not as badly affected. Rebuilding had begun gradually and with priority given to infrastructure and housing in less devastated parts of London, Tower Hamlets and other wards like it had moved further down on the priority list. Once works had commenced only very basic and cheap apartment blocks were built and several convenience kiosks. Overcrowding and illness were commonplace even today.

The tram station was a two minute walk from his destination. The driver gave Adam a curious look as he disembarked; even dressed as he was the heir to Larimore Systems was still easily recognisable.

The tram stop was alongside the former King Edward VII memorial park. The park was now little more than a grassy wasteland with a few saplings that had been planted in recent months. Adam walked alongside the park and down the street leading off from it to reach his destination.

Convenience kiosks were modern, dome-shaped shops that were a replacement to the traditional and vast supermarkets of the early and mid-twenty-first century. They were usually manned by four members of staff and were equipped with the latest security that was linked directly to the nearest police station. The kiosks mainly accepted payment cards although a few would take cash. The kiosks were normally about 600 square feet in size and stocked essential food and personal care items. There were also larger kiosks that stocked clothing and computers.

The kiosk was situated on the corner of the street flanked by an older apartment building. Outwardly the silver dome structure appeared no different from the others. Adam pressed the tile on the outside of the door to gain entrance.

Immediately to his left there was a stack of small, silver rectangular scanners that were used by customers. A sample of each product was displayed behind glass in the aisles with a unique code on the front of each case. The scanner would read this and ask the customer to confirm the quantity that they required. It also recorded a running total so customers could see just how much they had spent. Once they had finished customers took the scanner to the clerks. They would download the details of the products that the customer wanted to purchase onto the computer and the items were sorted in the secure storeroom at the rear of the kiosk. Only once the clerk had taken payment did customers receive their items.

Adam wasn't here to buy anything. He paused at the cash machine mounted on the right side wall and withdrew five hundred pounds, which was the maximum that he could withdraw at once, before making his way to the counter. The forty-something clerk glanced warily around and, once satisfied that none of the browsing customers were looking in their direction, motioned for Adam to follow him out to the storeroom. All the goods were stacked in crates and were labelled accordingly. There were narrow pathways leading between them and the clerk led Adam down one and to the back of the storeroom.

"We had some L.S.A agents looking around last week," the clerk told him quietly. "They didn't find anything, but as one of our more high-profile customers I thought you should know."

"Thanks," Adam replied appreciatively as he gave fifty pounds in cash to the clerk. Some of the other wealthy patrons might consider looking elsewhere for entertainment in case the kiosk was raided one night, but Adam didn't care if he was caught.

The man spent a few seconds counting the money before speaking again. "You know your way by now. Enjoy your night, Mr Larimore," he said as he pressed the tile to open the door.

Concealed tiles were hard to come by although they were easy to install without the need for a technician. These 'invisible' panels only came to life when direct pressure was applied and blended seamlessly into the rest of a wall. An 'invisible' doorway had become a necessity when the street entrance had been compromised. The white sliding panels were integrated into the wall and when closed it looked as though nothing was there. Only a very high-tech scanner could detect them.

Adam stepped through the door and started down the flight of steps directly in front of him. These led him to a second, soundproof door which opened electronically when he pressed his palm against the tile to release the lock.

Before the Great Tsunamis there had been a block of flats on this site. Despite the building being destroyed the basement had survived. In the months and years straight after the disaster it had been used as a shelter for survivors and a place to seek refuge from attacks during the war. Afterwards, and in the more recent times, it had served a very different purpose.

In the last thirty years underground, illegal nightclubs had become commonplace within the super cities. These clubs played loud music and served illegally produced alcohol. They were replicas of the clubs of the twenty-first century and Adam had been going to the one in old Tower Hamlets for over two years now.

The walls of the club were bare brick and old style lantern lights were mounted on them near to the ceiling. There were two security guards at the entrance. Neither gave him a second glance as he walked by. The bar and other furnishings were black and many of the fittings had been salvaged from the debris and remains of older buildings. There was dance floor at the back of the room.

"Hi Adam," Carl Cadman, the forty year old owner, greeted him as Adam sat down at the bar. "The usual?"

"Yeah thanks," Adam said as he handed Carl a wad of notes. "There's two hundred pounds here. Put it on tab for me."

Carl raised a dark eyebrow. "Celebrating?"

"My birthday."

"Many happy returns," he grinned as he set the double vodka down in front of Adam before moving down the bar to serve the next customer. Nowadays it was expensive to buy alcohol legitimately. Vodka and other spirits were subject to a forty percent Government tax due to limited production and even beers and lager that had been historically cheaper averaged at twenty pounds for a few cans. Part of this was also the environment tax on production of the packaging and also a bid by the Government to prevent drunken behaviour. So people turned to illegal establishments who made their own alcohol and soft drinks.

"I didn't expect to see you tonight," a low voice in his ear commented with ill-concealed surprise. Adam smiled and set the glass down as an arm wrapped around his waist.

Leon Durrand was three years older than Adam and was his lover. They had met in the club at the end of December. Leon worked at a factory producing clothing. It didn't pay well and he supplemented his income by selling Clarity. Clarity was the Ecstasy of the twenty-second century. Ironically it had first been created in an L.S.A laboratory, however, when its effects were discovered production was halted. Someone on the inside had sold details of its creation to the black market and now it was gaining popularity within illegal clubs. It was cheaper than its cousin and so catered perfectly to the poorer market. The name was misleading; it was a hallucinogenic first and foremost, combined with a sense of tranquillity and euphoria. Clarity had been its test name in the L.S.A labs, although the origin of this name was unknown. Adam had taken it a few times although he didn't really care for it.

"Father was displeased about what happened Friday night," he answered his lover with a grin. "I'm technically what used to be termed as 'grounded'."

Leon laughed as he slipped onto the vacant barstool beside him. Leon was only just taller than Adam and was slender with well-defined muscles. His hair was dyed blond and as he often cut it himself it had an almost rakish look to it. His eyes were dark brown and appeared somewhat unfeeling. Leon rarely expressed any emotions other than amusement and annoyance. He had several scars where he'd got into fights with contacts and addicts. Leon dressed casually in baggy trousers and loose fitting tops. He didn't care much for fashion and he didn't have the money for it in any case. There was a fine layer of stubble on his chin indicating that he hadn't shaved today. He was, to coin an old fashioned phrase, a 'bad boy'. Adam didn't care about that. It was partly what had attracted him to Leon in the first place.

Their relationship was kept casual as Leon didn't want anything serious. Until recently Adam had been happy with this. He could imagine what his father would do if he learned that his son and heir was gay. Adam knew that one day Victor would try to introduce him to the daughter of a wealthy business associate with the expectation that he would marry her and father a son to continue the family line. Adam grimaced at this thought. It was one conversation with his father that he dreaded. However, despite his concerns, gradually over the short time that he'd known Leon, Adam was realising that his feelings were starting to run deeper.

Leon signalled to Carl for the same again for Adam and one for himself.

"So your father doesn't know you're out?" he asked with a grin.

"He was under the impression that he could stop me," Adam answered as he took a drink from his second glass.

Leon sniggered and ran his free hand through his hair. "He's gonna be pissed when he finds you gone."

"Like I care," Adam replied. He didn't come here to talk about his father. "Want to dance?" he asked as he finished his drink.

"Sure," Leon agreed. Adam waited for his lover to drink the rest of his vodka before taking his hand and leading him onto the dance floor.

He pulled Leon into the crowd and immediately lost himself in the heavy rock music that was being played on the music system. He wasn't certain what era the music was from, but it was much better than the Government-funded rubbish that was produced nowadays. This was real music and Adam loved it. The vibrations from the thumping beat travelled up from the floor and through him, and that combined with the alcohol made him feel heady. Adrenaline rushed through him, fuelled when Leon wrapped an arm around his waist from behind and pulled Adam back against him. Tracks of music seemed to blur together and Adam wasn't sure how much time had gone by. They went to the bar so many times that Adam lost count, and they always made their way back onto the dance floor after finishing their drinks. Eventually when the beat of the current song slowed Adam felt Leon's palm that had been resting against his stomach casually slide underneath his top. Calloused fingers from years of manual work appreciatively brushed against his flawless skin.

"Do you want to get some air?" Leon murmured his suggestion against Adam's ear.

Adam had barely nodded before Leon was leading him across the floor and towards the exit.

The night was cool and not unwelcome after the stuffiness of the club, and the pleasant soak of alcohol in his system made Adam feel as though he were floating along. Leon's arm was draped around him and Adam pressed the side of his head into Leon's shoulder as they walked. He didn't even know where they were going and he doubted that Leon was entirely sure either. Adam was taken by surprise when Leon suddenly dragged him down an alley between two buildings and kissed him fiercely. Adam grunted more in shock than pain as his back hit the metal work. The cold seeped through the layer of his jacket and he shivered.

"Back to my place?" Leon suggested with a grin as he finally drew away.

Adam smirked and nodded in reply before kissing Leon again.

CHAPTER THREE

When Adam woke the next morning he had a thumping headache and his throat was almost painfully dry. The bed that he was lying in was a small single, which could barely accommodate the both of them. He could feel Leon pressed up against his back. Leon's left arm was draped loosely around his waist. Adam's face was about an inch from the off-white wall and the grey woven throw barely covered them. Adam closed his eyes again and turned over in Leon's arms so that he was lying against his lover's chest. A tiny part of him secretly relished these moments when he would wake up beside someone and feel arms around him. Then the moment was gone as he felt Leon stirring.

"Morning," the blond greeted him. "How's your head?"

"Pounding," Adam admitted with a soft laugh.

"Mine too. It was a great night though!"

"Yeah," Adam agreed. He studied the other man in silence for a few minutes. They got along well and the rapport they had fuelled Adam's hope that they might have a proper relationship in the future.

"Do you want to do something this morning?" Adam asked with some apprehension. He'd never vocalised his desire to spend some more time with his lover and he was unsure of how Leon might react to the suggestion.

"I've got work in a while," Leon replied almost immediately.

"Could you take the morning off?" Adam surprised both himself and Leon by asking. The annoyed sigh that Leon uttered in response made Adam immediately regret it.

"If I don't turn up they'll give my shifts away," he replied tersely.

"Oh."

As Adam's own job was pretty much secure for life he often forgot that for normal people it wasn't like that. Manual workers were treated poorly and if they were off sick then they would be replaced permanently.

"Why don't you come and work at Larimore Systems?" Adam suggested. It had been something he'd been thinking about for a while. Leon had a casual interest in computers and he had designed some custom games for the Eos system. With the right environment he could develop those skills and Adam knew that he disliked working at the factory. Leon's reaction, however, was not as positive as Adam had hoped.

"What would I do there? I'm not exactly a computer genius."

"There's a job vacancy in my Development Department. It's mainly checking software for glitches, but it will lead to other opportunities too."

This was a small lie; there was no job, however, Adam could hire whoever he wanted without the need for approval from his father or the board.

"I can't picture myself working somewhere like that," Leon replied disinterestedly.

"Fair enough," Adam shrugged. He kept his voice casual to hide his annoyance and some frustration that his offer had been turned down so quickly. "It would have been cool for us to have spent some more time together though."

Leon was silent for a moment. Even so the frown on his face clearly said what he was still thinking even before he voiced his thoughts.

"Adam, you know I'm not looking for a boyfriend."

"Nor am I!" Adam snapped sensitively. He drew away from Leon and sat up. The upset that he felt over this clarification made him feel defensive.

Leon pushed himself up and reached out to gently brush some strands of dark hair over Adam's bare shoulder.

"Don't get pissed, baby. I just needed to make sure we're still wanting the same thing here."

"We do. Nothing's changed," Adam half-heartedly reassured him. To reinforce this he turned around and wrapped an arm around Leon's shoulders, pulling the blond to him and crushing their mouths together in a heated kiss. Leon responded eagerly and pushed Adam back down onto his bed.

"I like you," he murmured when they parted for air. "And we have a good thing going here. Don't complicate things okay?"

"I'm not," Adam responded somewhat irately. He was embarrassed and just wanted to forget about the conversation. Leon had made his feelings perfectly clear. "When do you have to leave for work?"

Leon grinned. "Not for a little while," he replied.

***

Adam sighed as he turned the tap to halt the steady flow of lukewarm water that cascaded down onto him. Even though he had showered at Leon's before he'd never really got used to the manual operations that helped set the temperature, therefore his showers were usually mildly warm at best. Adam's shower at home was state-of-the-art and had computerised controls for temperature and also for setting the type of spray and even sound effects such as thunderstorms or a waterfall.

Adam stepped out of the cubicle and grabbed one of the towels on the rail opposite to dry himself with. He tied a second around his waist before exiting the room. Like in many of the poorer areas of the city Leon shared his flat with another family. In his case it was a couple and their daughter. The flat had two bedrooms and a communal kitchen and living space. The main bathroom was communal too, but as Leon's block was an older building some of the bedrooms had a very tiny en-suite. Leon's room was fortunate enough to have one, which Adam was thankful for as he didn't want too many people to see him here.

Leon had used the communal bathroom and was already dressed when Adam re-entered the bedroom. He was sitting at the small metal, glass-topped table in the corner of the room drinking from a mug of coffee. Since the war there had been no trading between countries and England had been forced to produce all its own food. This had resulted in years of hardship until the Government had the technology and ability to reintroduce proper and regular food production. To the very north of the country on the outskirts of the cities there were farms rearing livestock and growing plants, fruit and vegetables. At first production had proved very difficult with illness among the livestock and plants that were not supposed to be grown in the English climate dying. Then Government scientists had begun growing genetically modified crops that were better equipped to survive and even started breeding genetically engineered animals. In the past people had voiced serious concerns over the long-term health effects of consuming food produced in such a way, however, the nation was starving and had little choice.

"I've got to leave in a little while," Leon said as he sipped from his mug.

"Yeah I ought to get back anyway," Adam answered with a grimace as he thought about the wrath he would face when he did return home.

"So are you planning on going to the club next Saturday?"

"Depends," Adam replied with a grin.

"Tease," Leon grumbled good-naturedly.

Adam merely smirked as they both finished their coffee. Leon then watched in amusement as Adam attempted to locate his clothing. He found his jeans and briefs at the foot of the bed. His new top was over by the door and he felt some momentary dismay when he found a tear down the left hand side and another through the black netting.

Leon grinned as they both recalled how much trouble they'd had removing that particular item of clothing last night. Adam smiled, dismissing the damage as he pulled on Leon's shirt instead. He found his boots and socks partly under Leon's bed. His jacket was lying by the door.

After he had got dressed and they were ready to leave, Leon suddenly pushed Adam up against the closed door and kissed him. Adam relaxed into the embrace, wrapping one arm around Leon's shoulders whilst his other entangled itself in Leon's hair.

"I finish work at nine tonight," Leon murmured when they parted. "Just so you know."

Adam smiled. "I'll keep that in mind." He wondered if this was a hint that Leon wanted to spend more time with him than he was prepared to voice directly. The idea gave Adam fresh hope that there might be a chance of more to their relationship. Recalling Leon's reaction earlier made him wary about approaching the subject again so Adam decided against it. Leon kissed him again briefly before they left the apartment. As it was still early there was no one about and they made it outside without running into anyone.

"You going to be all right getting back?" Leon asked when they reached the crossroad in the street.

"Yeah. I might have a walk around first. It'll piss father and Eleanor off more if I don't turn up until this afternoon!"

Leon sniggered. "So tonight then?"

As he spoke Adam caught sight of a Government marked car turning onto their street. He shook his head. "Might have to leave it until the weekend."

"Yeah?" Leon eyed the vehicle warily.

"You'd better take off," Adam advised.

The blond agreed. "See you later."

Adam nodded, trying to keep his expression casual as Leon hurried away from him and down the next street.

Adam sighed as the car pulled up beside him. It was chrome-coloured and was top of the range. It was driven automatically by an inbuilt touch screen computer. A steering wheel remained, which made manual operation possible although most people chose the automatic option. Data was fed directly into it from the central Government database as were maps of all the cities. The leather seats were set quite far back from the windscreen and there was room for one passenger in the front. The back of the car was used for detainees.

The automatic window slid down to reveal Ivan. "I've been looking for you for hours," he told Adam as he opened the passenger door.

Adam shrugged. "Do I care?"

"Your father is furious," Ivan pointed out.

"So what? Isn't he always with me?"

"This has to stop, Adam."

The younger man laughed and shook his head. "Now you're starting to sound like him."

"Please can you get into the car so we can talk properly?"

"I didn't think you cared."

"Your father is my best friend and you're my godson. Of course I care, Adam. Please get in the car."

"Fine," Adam relented and did as he was asked.

"Where were you last night?" Ivan questioned with some concern as he sat down.

"Celebrating my birthday."

"Where?"

"Does it matter? I didn't get into any trouble again, Ivan."

"I know," the older man said patiently, "but that isn't the point. I can help you, Adam."

"I don't need any help."

"So you're happy with how things are?"

Adam didn't reply and slouched down in his seat. He put his feet up on the dashboard as the car pulled away from the pavement. He remained silent for the journey. Adam had known that his father would be furious although a part of him had hoped that Victor would have been worried about his son.

"Adam," Ivan tried again as the car stopped outside of Venewood. "You need to start turning things around. I cannot continue to cover for you. It is jeopardising my position and future prospects."

The younger man laughed scornfully at this. "So all you care about is your precious promotion?"

"Do you want to go to prison?" Ivan countered.

Adam frowned. He didn't.

"You're an exceptionally smart and talented young man. You can do anything you want. Larimore Systems is not it for you."

"What do you mean?" Adam asked curiously as he took his feet off of the dashboard.

"One day you will inherit your father's company, but you do not have to devote your life to it. Have you ever thought of joining the L.S.A? I believe that they could certainly benefit from your computer and programming skills."

"Wouldn't that conflict with Larimore Systems?" Adam asked. He feigned disinterest although in reality he was rather intrigued. The Government purchased technology produced by Larimore Systems for the L.S.A. Surely they couldn't be interested in creating their own?

"I'm sure we can work around that. As you know Jeff Ingham will be stepping down at the end of the year. As it stands I will be his successor and I intend to run things rather differently."

"What did you have in mind?"

"There are a number of projects that I would like to start,

however, their current Chief Technician does not possess the skill set that I require."

"And why do you think I would be better suited?"

"You are very focused, calm under pressure, able to think on your feet and talk yourself out of any situation imaginable. These are some of the traits required of L.S.A agents."

Adam struggled to conceal his surprise at this. He could hardly picture himself in gunfights or on secret operations into hostile territories.

"I'm not exactly Eric Rawlins," he pointed out in amusement. Eric Rawlins was the L.S.A's best agent. Like Adam he was genetically engineered although he was given more physical attributes such as strength which enabled the L.S.A to fashion him into a superhero. A lot of it was a publicity stunt, but it worked and the L.S.A's popularity had increased in the last five or so years thanks to Eric. Adam had never met him, but he had seen footage of him in the Information Bank files. He looked like he was a decent guy albeit somewhat naïve. And he was very handsome. He rather resembled a hero from the old films of the past with his muscular build and clean cut good looks. His hair was brown and unruly. He had friendly mocha eyes and a shy smile that endeared him to much of the population; male and female. Adam certainly wouldn't turn the guy down. Eric had a long-term girlfriend, Bex Vixen, who also happened to be his partner out in the field.

"That's not what I'm proposing," Ivan shook his head, cutting into Adam's thoughts.

"Then what are you proposing?" Adam asked with interest.

"That you would be quite an asset to the L.S.A. It is an excellent opportunity, Adam. And, between us, if you are so determined to make a point to your father this is a much better way of going about it."

"I'll think about it, Ivan," Adam replied as he got out of the car. "Thanks for the ride."

"Please keep in mind all that I've just said," Ivan called after him as Adam walked towards his home. As he opened the door and stepped over the threshold, Adam saw that his father and Joseph were waiting for him.

Adam hated Joseph and the feeling was more than mutual. Joseph was smart and currently held a junior position at Larimore Systems with the hope of a promotion in future years. Not if Adam had anything to do with it and they both knew it. Joseph took after his father, who had died when he was a child. He was a good few inches taller than Adam. He was strong and more athletic than he used to be thanks to hourly workout sessions in their private gymnasium each day. Joseph wasn't attractive. His eyes were small and too close together. He had a mop of thinning light brown hair and Adam predicted that he would be bald by the time he reached thirty-five. The sneer in his smile he had inherited from his mother and it was often directed at Adam. The two of them fought behind Victor's back and Joseph tried to keep close to his stepfather most likely in the hopes that he would give him a position of better standing within Larimore Systems. As much as this infuriated Adam at times he reminded himself that when he finally inherited the company his first act would be to fire Joseph.

"Where the hell have you been?" his father demanded furiously. "I expressly forbade you from leaving this house."

"I got bored," Adam said indifferently as he brushed past his father and headed for the stairs.

“How dare you show such disrespect? I am your father!”

Angrily the older man followed him and seized hold of his arm. Adam winced as he was roughly jerked back into the lobby. All the while Joseph remained silent. He stared coldly at Adam as the scene played out.

“Answer my question!” Victor snapped as his grip on Adam’s arm tightened. “Where have you been?”

“Just out celebrating my birthday. I didn’t get into any trouble and Ivan drove me home. You can ask him if you don’t believe me.”

“Believe me I will, Adam. As punishment you are suspended from Larimore Systems for a further month. Now get out of my sight.”

Adam tentatively rubbed at his arm when his father released his grip. He was somewhat surprised that he had got off this lightly, but what could his father do? There was no point in preventing Adam from leaving the house; he could easily get around the security system again. He glanced back over his shoulder at the older man and smirked before starting to climb the stairs. However, Adam’s smug expression soon faded when he realised that Joseph was following him. He quickened his pace in the hope that he would reach his room before his stepbrother caught up with him. Whilst Adam was not afraid of him, he had not liked the dark look in his eyes.

Joseph had anticipated this and hurried after him. Adam had barely made it to the top of the staircase before he felt Joseph’s hands on his shoulders. He was shoved forwards and into the wall. Joseph pressed his right forearm across Adam’s upper back to stop him from pushing away whilst his other hand grabbed a fistful of his hair and jerked Adam’s head back at a painful angle.

"You may not care what effect your antics are having on our company, but I do and this stops now. Because of your suspension many projects will be set back months, possibly a year, and father will lose a lot of money."

"*Our* company?" Adam hissed through gritted teeth. "Father only allows your input because it makes Eleanor happy. One day that company will be mine and the first thing I am going to do is throw you out on your ass. You and that gold digging bitch!"

Adam knew what kind of reaction his words would have, but the sheer nerve of the other man had made him see red.

Joseph growled something inaudible under his breath before striking Adam round the back of the head. The younger man's vision momentarily darkened after the impact. Joseph had now released his grip on his stepbrother. Adam drew in a deep breath as he squeezed his eyes shut in a bid to will off the pain. When the stinging was tolerable Adam turned around and gathered himself enough for a counter blow. This his stepbrother was not expecting. Adam felt vague satisfaction when his fist connected with Joseph's nose. The crunch of cartilage and the yell of pain that followed was immensely satisfying. Joseph staggered backwards, his left hand covering his face. Crimson seeped between his fingers and dripped onto the floor. Adam smirked as his stepbrother contemplated retaliation. However, the bedroom door at the end of the hallway opened and put paid to this.

"Joe?" Eleanor's hand flew to her mouth in horror when she saw that her precious boy was bleeding. "What's he done to you?"

Eleanor often complained of migraines and as she was only wearing her nightgown Adam supposed she must have been suffering from one this morning. Eleanor raced down the hall towards them. She wrapped an arm around her son's shoulders and began guiding him towards the bathroom.

"Victor!" she shouted as they went. "Please call for the medics. The boys have had another disagreement."

Adam sighed and leaned back against the wall as his father began to ascend the stairs.

"What have you done now?" he demanded of Adam once he reached the top.

"He started it, father."

Victor scowled and followed the other two into the bathroom. "Is it broken?" Adam heard him ask.

"I think so," Eleanor answered worriedly. "We ought to call for a medic to be sure."

Emergency medical treatment was a Government service and one that invoked a hefty charge if the injury didn't warrant a call out. The Larimore's wealth meant that they did not have to worry about any charges. If a family who could not pay the charge called them and it wasn't deemed an emergency they would still come out but a charge would be deducted automatically from the wages of all working family members until the debt was paid in full. If there was an accident then the party who caused it would pay or face jail time.

"Adam, call for a medic," his father called out irately. "This is just great. We have a presentation to the L.S.A and the Government tomorrow afternoon and he's going to look like he got into a common brawl!"

Adam sniggered as he made his way into his bedroom to make the call. Victories over Joseph when they had a physical confrontation were rare and Adam wanted to savour this moment. Especially as it looked as though he'd managed to ruin things for his stepbrother tomorrow too.

CHAPTER FOUR

"So to conclude, the Ares II software upgrade for the defence system will allow you to control individual shields from anywhere in the country through our secure program. The encryption security feature can be locked to just a single user if one so desires. Ares II also eradicates imperfections in the current system and can be installed in full within three to four hours." Adam glanced up at the men sitting before him as he finished the presentation. Prime Minister Max Roberts was seated at the centre of the metal table. To his left was Jeff Ingham, the Head of the L.S.A, and to his right Simon Matheson, the L.S.A's Chief Technician. Much to Joseph's displeasure Adam had been asked to give the presentation with his father instead. Despite him being suspended from Larimore Systems, Victor would rather have Adam there than explain Joseph's broken nose to the most important men in the country. Victor had agreed to the development of the Ares II software in advance of the contract being finalised. This was a risky strategy, but seeing as the L.S.A already used their Ares

I system, Adam didn't consider this a difficult deal to close. Money would be the only possible issue; as it always was with the Government. Whilst they had no qualms about high taxes, they were reluctant to spend more than they had to.

"Do you have any questions?" Adam added as an afterthought when he saw the rather concerned looks on several faces in the room.

"How much does it cost?" Prime Minister Roberts asked. He was always to the point where money was concerned. He was in his late sixties and it was expected that he would retire at some point within the next year or so. Adam wondered if ill-health was also playing a part. He had been a larger man early on in his career, however, over the last six months he had lost a lot of weight. Roberts made few public appearances now and often seemed tired.

Further fuelling the speculation was the presence of his potential successor; Thomas Sherrin. Sherrin was a polar opposite of Prime Minister Roberts. A younger man, in his mid-thirties he was slim and had the gift of charisma. He appealed to every generation and always knew exactly what to say and in the right way, even if the news was bad. His appearance could be described as 'trendy'. Unlike most politicians he chose to keep his brown hair longer and in the modern feathered style that had regained popularity in the last few years. He knew enough youthful terminology to appeal to younger people. Sherrin also presented a softer edge when dealing with sensitive and difficult subjects. In Adam's mind this meant that there was no question of his succession. His position was as much assured as Ivan's.

The voting system had been internalised after the war and only the Government and others considered important enough to vote were given a say. The first Government had defended the new system by saying it created a more stable country as before the war and tsunamis there were too many political parties all with different policies and agendas. This meant that every time there was a new regime the goals changed. For example there could have been more funding for public medical care under one Government, but if they lost power to another who spent less on healthcare then there was a decline in the quality of the service. This way made everything consistent, or so they said. Adam, however, was more of the opinion that the new system was closer to a dictatorship than a democracy and he was sure that he wasn't the only one who thought so.

"Five hundred thousand pounds per installation per city," Adam answered Roberts' question without hesitating. He was aware that some of the people in the room had grown uncomfortable at such a high price being confirmed.

"The cost of not having the software would be more," Adam's father added.

"Couldn't we just pay for Adam's time and he could update the Ares I system?" Jeff Ingham proposed in a bid to save some money.

"It would be more cost effective to purchase the new software," Adam swiftly clarified for them. "Ares I is out of date and is already behind America in the terms of functionality."

That would give them something to think about. America's recovery after the war had been faster than England's. The possibility of an attack always made them anxious.

"You are certain that Ares II is secure?" Matheson queried. "Ares I had a backdoor program that could have potentially been manipulated had I not made adjustments to the software myself."

"Ares I was designed by an experienced team, however, it was not designed for the purpose that the L.S.A uses it for. Ares II was made to specification," Adam answered him.

"How can you be certain that it is one hundred percent secure?" Matheson pressed.

"Because I designed Ares II myself," Adam responded with a degree of smugness. "No one can get through the security system. You have my personal guarantee of this."

Matheson nodded, appearing satisfied. There was no reason that he wouldn't be. After all any program designed by Adam Larimore was one hundred percent hack proof.

Simon Matheson had held his position as Chief Technician for over twenty years. He was considered an expert in his field although he was an amateur compared to Adam. In previous encounters Adam had been given the impression that Matheson didn't like him; that he thought Adam was arrogant and full of himself. But why wouldn't he be? As far as computer programming went Adam was the best. No one else even came close, and Adam was pretty sure that Matheson was aware of this.

Matheson seemed to be somewhat of a worrier and often took off his glasses and cleaned the lenses when he was agitated by something. He had done so now; his eyes were bloodshot and the dark marks under them indicated that he had been working late. This was most likely by choice as he had no wife and child to go home to. He was solidly built without being overweight. His clothes were rumpled and his brown hair tussled as though he often forgot to run a comb through it. Adam could understand why Ivan had wanted Adam's input into his new projects over Matheson's. The man was good at his job, but he had no real passion for the role. Matheson was content to merely do what was required of him whilst Adam enjoyed re-writing software and developing his own.

A few further questions drew Adam from his musings; these were mainly concerning finance and timescales so Adam was content to sit down and let his father field them. It was sad as they did make a good team, Adam thought to himself before swiftly crushing this. It was what his father had wanted after all. To have an heir whom he could work alongside with. That was all he cared about.

"Thank you very much for your time, gentlemen," Victor was finishing now. "I will email you all copies of the program manuals for you to look over. If you have any queries in the meantime please contact me."

They would be left to pack up the presentation and then a private L.S.A vehicle would take them home. Adam knew this routine by heart now. However, this time things took a different turn.

"We have a slight problem with our archive footage," Ingham said to Adam as they were leaving. "Can you take a look at it? I will arrange for a car to take you home afterwards."

It was quite clear that Ingham wanted to speak to him without his father present. In any case Victor was keen to get back and wasn't paying attention to any underlying meanings.

"Of course," Adam nodded in agreement.

"I'll see you back at home," his father said curtly as he hurried after the Prime Minister and his security in the hopes of putting in a further good word for his company.

The meeting room was on Level 2 of the L.S.A

headquarters. Adam had memorised the different levels on his first visit and he wasn't surprised when Ingham dismissed Matheson and led Adam down the corridor to his office instead. Adam wasn't sure what Ingham's background was originally, although he wouldn't be surprised if it was military; he had that authoritative edge to him. He was in his sixties now and his expected retirement was a much discussed topic within the Government departments and general population itself. Ingham appeared slightly older than his years; the little hair he had left was already completely grey and so was his neatly trimmed beard. The slight yellowish tinge to his skin indicated the onset of liver disease, most likely caused by excessive drinking. Adam wouldn't be surprised in his line of work. Everyone needed an outlet for stress after all.

"Would you like something to drink?" Ingham offered as he gestured for Adam to sit down. The office was quite impersonal and furnished completely in chrome. The inbuilt computer in the desk was flashing and a few presses to different parts of the screen from Ingham put it into sleep mode.

"I'm fine, thank you," Adam replied as he made himself comfortable. He leaned back in the chair and met Ingham's gaze. "I assume you don't want to talk to me about the archive footage?"

"No. I had a meeting with Ivan Williams this morning and I understand from him that you have expressed an interest in joining the L.S.A?"

Adam chuckled to himself. Leave it to Ivan to put a spin on things so any potential backlash wouldn't have an effect on him! "I didn't put it quite like that, but your organisation does intrigue me."

Ingham smiled. "Should I take that as a compliment?"

"If you like," Adam smirked.

The Head of the L.S.A held Adam's gaze for a moment longer before speaking again. "Unfortunately your many personal problems mean that at this current time you would not be a good fit for our organisation."

Adam smiled thinly. This was hardly surprising to him. Only Ivan would think to give him a chance. "Well," he shrugged casually as though the older man's bluntness did not bother him, "as you clearly haven't invited me here to discuss a job offer, can I ask why you wanted to speak to me alone?"

Ingham smiled, clearly appreciating Adam getting straight to the point. "A lot of the files on the current Ares I server are confidential. There are many that can only be accessed by myself and select senior staff. Despite the Prime Minister's concerns regarding the cost I am certain that the order for Ares II will be approved. I have asked you here to request that when you upgrade the system that those files are moved to a separate folder that only specific individuals can access. Will you personally oversee this?"

The request was quite a standard one and it seemed a little odd that Ingham would want to speak to Adam specifically regarding it.

"Are the files secure?"

"Yes," Ingham nodded. "They're all locked to user ID and password. Is this going to be a problem?"

"Not at all. I can transfer them without the need for access."

"I will also need you to ensure that the originals are irreversibly wiped from the old Ares I computers once the transfer is complete."

"That is standard procedure," Adam confirmed. He wanted to ask Ingham exactly why he was so concerned about the files that he would want to speak to Adam confidentially, but something warned him against it. All Government agencies had their secrets and Adam figured there was a fair few in those files. He was also sure that had there been anyone else to make this request to then Ingham would have spoken to them instead. Adam knew that they viewed him as somewhat an unreliable ally and only had business dealings with him because he was the best programmer in England, if not the world. They had no choice and this didn't mean that they trusted him.

"Once the date for installation has been confirmed arrange for me to come in a few hours before. We can discuss the finer points then. How does that sound?"

"Good. Thank you. You will also need to sign a non-disclosure agreement."

"Why?" Adam asked in some surprise. "I'm not accessing the files."

"I realise that," Ingham's attempt at a friendly smile definitely had a colder edge to it now. His steely blue gaze held Adam's own as he continued. "Those files contain sensitive and highly classified information. If you were to accidently become privy to some of the information I would need a guarantee that you wouldn't use the information in a way that might negatively affect the L.S.A's interests."

"Larimore Systems handles requests such as these all the time," Adam assured him without even reacting to the underlying threat in Ingham's tone. "I can assure you that no access to any file or document will be made. However, I am happy to sign your agreement if it makes you feel more comfortable."

Ingham clearly didn't like Adam's nonchalant response, however, he chose not to be drawn by it.

"Good," he replied simply and stood to indicate that their conversation was over. "I will arrange for a car to take you home."

***

"You weren't very long," Victor commented when Adam arrived back home. He and his wife were in the living room. Victor was seated in a chair whilst Eleanor was sprawled out across the sofa. She barely glanced up at Adam and kept most of her attention on her handheld computer. Her lips were pursed giving an indication of her annoyance. She clearly felt that Joseph should have been the one to give the presentation with her husband. Adam's stepbrother had gone into the office today instead and wouldn't be back until later on. The two of them had hardly spoken and Adam didn't doubt that Joseph would retaliate for what had happened yesterday. It wasn't in his nature to just let things go.

"It was a minor problem with the system," Adam answered disinterestedly as his gaze fell to the half empty bottle of wine on the coffee table in front of Eleanor.

"You've started early," he said pointedly.

"That's the effect you have on us all, Adam dear," the blonde answered sweetly.

Victor shot Adam a dirty look and then turned his attention back to the computer in his hand. Adam gave them a look of disgust in return before going upstairs to his room. He picked up his portable computer from his desk. Adam switched it on and sat down on his bed as he mulled over his conversation with Jeff Ingham. Adam was used to handling clients' confidential information, and Government information, but there was something very different about this request. Ingham had seemed agitated about the prospect of the files being accessed during the system upgrade. It was very intriguing to say the least.

Adam opened his email application and discovered one new message from Ivan. He was asking how the meeting had gone and if Adam had given their conversation regarding the L.S.A any further thought.

Despite Ivan's proposition being interesting, Adam wasn't certain that he wanted to work for someone. Why on Earth would he when he would inherit his own company? It would piss his father off though, which *did* appeal to him.

Adam lay back on his bed with his computer still in hand. He called up the Information Bank and opened it on the L.S.A's website. A lot of it was designed for the public. The welcome page had a photograph of Eric Rawlins and Bex Vixen along with details of their latest successful rescue aiding some workers who had been trapped when a building collapsed on the outskirts of Sector Four. Only these positive and public appealing stories made it into the Information Bank. However, as Larimore Systems provided the technology for the Government and L.S.A, Adam had more of an idea of what went on. There were fractious individuals who resented the post-tsunami England and yearned for the ways of the past. They occasionally attacked and killed L.S.A operatives or Government officials. Part of the L.S.A's job was to root out these individuals and silence them. There were also attempts by foreign hostiles to attack the defence shields or infiltrate the country from the coast. There was a darker side to every organisation, Adam supposed, although he would be interested to learn just how far the L.S.A was prepared to go.

The Information Bank did not really tell Adam a lot that he didn't already know and he closed the site down. Instead he occupied himself by playing a couple of games. They really only held his interest for half an hour at the most each as he could easily complete them with the aid of cheats and hacks. His username, Erebus2115, was the current high scorer on every game that he had played. As much as it gave him a sense of smug satisfaction, sometimes Adam longed for a real challenge. Likewise with people; he had never met anyone who could get the better of him. Whilst that idea was less appealing, Adam would be intrigued to meet his equal.

"Adam?" he glanced up when his bedroom door slid open. "I've just heard from Jeff Ingham. The Prime Minister would like to purchase Ares II for the L.S.A," Victor said. "I have arranged with Mr Ingham for you to visit the L.S.A headquarters on Monday for installation."

"I thought I was suspended?" Adam queried. He'd known when discussing the program with Ingham that he would be the one to install it. Adam and his father both knew that this was too important a contract to delegate to anyone else in the company.

"You will do this without pay," his father answered sternly. "Mr Ingham has arranged for a vehicle to pick you up at 9.30am. You will also be required to train several L.S.A staff in using the new system."

"Do they realise that training is extra?"

"They do. I have emailed you the list of staff. Some of

them are not as computer literate as Simon Matheson so you will need to keep this in mind when you are preparing."

"I've done this before," Adam pointed out in irritation as he opened the email and quickly scanned the list of staff. The three he knew were Jeff Ingham, Simon Matheson and Rebecca 'Bex' Vixen. The other two, Nate Rowland and Susan Li, he'd not even heard of by name. He was surprised, and a little disappointed, that Eric Rawlins was not on the list, but the L.S.A most likely had better uses for his time.

"Just ensure that everything goes smoothly on Monday," his father said as he turned to exit the bedroom. "And Joseph will be accompanying you."

"What?" Adam demanded as he sat up. "Father, I do not need—"

"He was very disappointed not to be able to present with me today and as it was your fault you will tolerate his presence. Joseph will certainly tell me if you do any different."

"Fine," Adam sighed and turned his attention back to his computer. Victor murmured something inaudible under his breath before leaving the room.

CHAPTER FIVE

Ares I security mainframe version 1.5. Enter password to continue

Adam crossed off the warning screen and entered various commands on the touchscreen until a blue box appeared.

Run metis/AresI/override/

After entering this the computer immediately responded and seconds later the blue background was replaced with the L.S.A server screen. Adam smirked to himself. Hacking into the Ares I system had been much easier than he had anticipated.

It was Saturday afternoon and his father was attending an afternoon drinks and dinner that one of his rich friends was holding in Sector Two. Eleanor and Joseph had accompanied him. Adam had not been permitted to due to his recent behaviour and he couldn't care less really. This was far more interesting.

With his conversation with Ingham and also Ivan's proposal capturing Adam's interest in the L.S.A, he had resisted temptation for as long as possible. However, Adam couldn't hold back his curiosity any longer. He wanted to find out exactly what they got up to and why Ingham was so agitated about his files being moved.

Adam already had basic remote access to the system through Larimore Systems, but he was not going to risk getting caught using the company system for hacking a Government agency. Instead he had created a program on his personal computer that prevented anyone from tracing the origin of the intrusion. Adam had designed all the software on his computer himself and it was unique. He called the system Aether. It was only in the beta stage and so far it had proved far more reliable than the Eos system that he had developed for Larimore Systems. Aether, however, Adam wanted to keep separate. It was Aether that he used to circumvent the security systems installed in their home and on his father's computer. Adam certainly didn't want his father, or Joseph, getting hold of it. Getting into the L.S.A's system was a bigger test for Aether than the security at home and Adam felt rather smug that he had managed this so easily.

He opened up a couple of top level folders detailing various documentation concerning the L.S.A. Much of it was already available on the Information Bank. Adam sifted through this for a couple of minutes before going deeper into the system.

The funding for the L.S.A was extremely high, much higher than had publically been released. This was unsurprising. It was how the finances were being distributed that was interesting. A lot of money was being poured into the L.H.A.G.S – the London Hospital of Advanced Genetic Sciences. The L.H.A.G.S was situated in Sector Four and was the main genetic research facility in England. There were also copies of the L.H.A.G.S files on the L.S.A's system. It was at the L.H.A.G.S where the designer babies were created. Where he had been created. Adam swallowed hard. He suspected that if he dug deep enough the file containing the details of his creation was here. Adam opened a file that listed the approved parents and their selections for the current year. Most were normal people and so only hair and eye colour selection had been added as standard. Two sets of names Adam recognised as people who worked for Larimore Systems. They had also paid for a couple of additional traits. It was disgusting Adam thought to himself. Whereas he could see the logic in wanting to produce from the best possible gene pool whilst England was still recovering, people were now becoming technology. Things to be used for the gains of others. Adam certainly felt that way most of the time. The perfect child was now a reality and yet parents were disappointed when that child turned out to be anything less.

It was strange Adam thought to himself as he read through a few of the files. Some of them were highlighted in red. There seemed to be no explanation for this. Adam closed them down and searched further through the list of folders. There were some hidden folders that were only viewable to those senior employees with complete access to the system. Those had to be the folders and files that Ingham was talking about. The folders were login and password protected as Ingham had said, but it took Adam less than two minutes to gain access. The folder that first drew his eye was entitled 'Population Growth and Control Plan'. There was a single document inside the folder that was marked 'classified'. This had additional security that Adam was just as easily able to circumvent.

The document was twenty pages long and was titled **'Population growth and control plan: 2062. Updated version 2099-2119'**

Adam frowned as he continued to read.

In order to ensure the security and safety of the nation, the Government has discussed and agreed the following mandates for the London Security Agency in respect of population growth within the capital. This plan mirrors those set out within other major cities to guarantee continuity.

When reading this paper please note the following:

I. The below plan sets out the target population growth rates for the capital and also the projected mortality rate.

II. The specifications for genetic engineering are intended to be a guide and final decisions regarding specifications are to be taken by the appointed L.S.A agents and the appropriately qualified senior medical staff of the L.H.A.G.S.

III. Senior officials are advised to take note of the mortality rates in their individual sectors.

IV. The Government reserves the right to directly overrule or amend a specification.

V. Specification decisions made by senior officials are final unless IV above applies.

1. Selection

1.1 Prospective parents are interviewed and assessed according to the following criteria:

1.1.1 Class

1.1.2 Finance

1.1.3 Health

1.1.4 Ward

1.1.5 Other significant factors

1.2 If the above criteria has been met then senior officials and doctors will meet with the prospective parents to agree the specification and/or other specifications as permitted in relation to 1.1.2 above.

Note 1: *Predisposed genetic conditioning will be decided after 1.2 takes place. Factors as set out at 1.1 above will be taken into consideration.*

Note 2: *Senior officials will have final authority regarding Note 1 above unless IV in the introductory pages applies.*

2. Predisposed Genetic Conditioning

Predisposed genetic conditioning is designed to prevent the over-population of the city, specifically in overcrowded or poorer wards. Selection for predisposed genetic conditioning is decided based on parentage, the area in which prospective parents live and the criteria specified in 1.1 above. Note: Note 2 and IV above apply in all cases.

2.1 Specification of predisposed genetic conditioning

Predisposed genetic conditioning specification is the process whereby selected embryos are predisposed to cancer and other genetic disorders. Predisposed genetic conditioning is designed to maintain a sustainable population and moderate growth in certain areas.

2.2 Predisposed genetic conditioning and the Government

The decision to introduce predisposed genetic conditioning was made in September 2062 when the economic advisers produced their reports indicating that population recovery would be swifter than the country could afford. The decision allows for moderated growth as well as ensuring that poorer areas do not become overcrowded. The Government tasked the L.S.A with overseeing the process, which has proved successful to date (date of report 2099).

Adam was disgusted and stunned by what he was reading. Skimming down to a few paragraphs he also read that calmer traits and lower IQs were preferable in poor or middle class babies. Affluent potential parents, such as his father, were exempt from the predisposed genetic conditioning process and were essentially permitted as many modifications as they could afford. Adam sat silently for a while as he struggled to come to terms with all of this. How could the officials even contemplate doing this? Adam had known that the Government and L.S.A manipulated the media and public thinking, but deliberately engineering babies to die…it sickened Adam. They sentenced thousands of people to die before their time and all because they wanted to retain control of the population. He thought of his own creation and birth. He was healthy and free all because of who his father was.

Adam downloaded the documents onto his own computer and ensured that they were encrypted so only he could access them. Adam also downloaded personnel files for senior L.S.A staff and agents. Jeff Ingham, unsurprisingly, was head of the programme and met with the Prime Minister once every few months to discuss this and financial matters.

As much as the information horrified him, Adam had no idea what he was going to do with it. He recalled the very clear threat that Ingham had made yesterday. If Adam told anyone then, from reading what he just had, he was certain that he'd be silenced. He wondered if Ivan knew or whether it was something that only newly appointed Heads of the L.S.A were told. Adam knew that he couldn't just do nothing with this information, but he had to think his next move through carefully. If he told the wrong person then he could end up in prison, or at the bottom of the Thames.

It was nearly eight when Adam finished reading all the files that he had downloaded. The Government and L.S.A were corrupt to the core and even if he had seriously been contemplating Ivan's offer there was no possible way he could accept it now.

Then the call icon on his computer started flashing and distracted him from his thoughts. Adam smiled when he saw the caller ID; Leon. Adam had forgotten that he'd said that he would be at the club tonight. He had to admit that he was pleased that Leon would miss him enough to call.

"Hey Adam," the blond greeted him when he pressed the icon to accept the call. He was out on the street opposite the kiosk that housed the club. "I'm getting kind of lonely. Are you on your way?"

"I don't really feel like going to the club tonight." Adam replied reluctantly. He really ought to stay here and try to decide what he was going to do with what he had learned.

Leon frowned in annoyance. "Why not?"

"I'm not in the mood, that's all," Adam snapped a little defensively.

"God, you're so boring," the blond sighed. "I guess I'll just go on my own then."

The boring remark stung and Adam scowled at his lover as he reconsidered. What could he do about the L.S.A right this minute anyway? The information was a lot for anyone to take in and, as well as welcoming a distraction to take his mind off of it, Adam really wanted to see Leon.

"Why don't I come over to yours instead?" Adam suggested.

Immediately Leon's annoyance faded and he smirked as

he replied. "Sure. I'll head home and see you there."

"No, wait for me where you are."

"Why?" Leon asked with interest.

Adam grinned. "You'll see," he promised before ending the call. He'd show Leon that Adam Larimore was certainly not boring.

He closed down his computer and hurriedly changed into a pair of black jeans and a ripped black tank top before heading downstairs and out of the front door. On the pavement outside the house was the car that Adam's father had given Joseph for his birthday. Adam stared at the vehicle and smirked. Taking the car was certainly going to liven up their evening and would piss Joseph off at the same time.

***

"Nice ride!" Leon commented as Adam pulled up beside him. It had been easy to hack into the computer and override the system for a manual drive. Even though Adam had not driven a car before he'd soon got the hang of it. Driving round the city wasn't easy though as the streets had been rebuilt with mainly tram and pedestrian use in mind. A separate lane that was specifically for vehicles ran alongside the tram lanes in the main streets, however, this was rarely used as cars were not as commonplace as they had been in the last century.

He took a swig from the bottle of vodka that he'd bought from home and then offered it to Leon as he climbed into the car.

Leon grinned as he took a longer drink before setting the bottle down on the floor at his feet. He then leaned over to kiss Adam. "Shall we go back to my apartment?" he suggested as he ran a hand down Adam's bare left arm.

"Later," Adam replied as he drew back. "I want to go for a drive first."

"Sounds good to me," Leon answered with another grin.

Adam pressed the button on the touch screen that put the car into drive and pulled it away from the side of the street. He selected eighty miles per hour on the speed controls and deselected the auto-slow for turning corners. The streets were deserted and appeared to flash by.

"How fast can it go?" Leon asked as he took another drink from the bottle of vodka.

Adam shrugged and checked the console. "Hundred and twenty miles per hour," he replied.

"This is fucking awesome! Where did you get it?"

"It's my stepbrother's."

"Does he mind you borrowing it?"

"I didn't ask! Would you like to drive for a bit?"

"Sure!"

Adam pulled over long enough for them to change seats. "The computer sets the speed and changes the gears automatically. All you have to do is steer and brake."

"How much does one of these set you back?" Leon asked.

Adam shrugged. "This is state-of-the-art so I'd say almost half a million."

"Fuck! Your stepbrother will be pissed then!"

"Do you think I care about that?" Adam drank the rest of the vodka and tossed the bottle out of the open window. He leaned back in the seat and shut his eyes as he felt the coolness of the evening breeze on his skin. He almost regretted looking at those files now. There were some things that, Adam reasoned, you were better off not knowing.

He was jolted out of his thoughts when Leon stopped the car. Adam opened his eyes, although he barely had time to focus on his surroundings when Leon leaned across the gap that separated them. He kissed Adam tentatively at first as they were in public. Adam was mildly concerned that someone might see them, but he forced this to the back of his mind as he returned the kiss just as keenly as he did when they were alone. As Leon's hand slid under his tank top Adam reached over into the gap between the two seats and pressed the button that caused the passenger seat to recline backwards.

"Whoa!" Leon wasn't expecting this. He lost his balance and fell on top of Adam. Adam sniggered as Leon pushed himself back up. "Here then?" he questioned with some amusement.

"Yeah," Adam nodded, not breaking Leon's gaze.

The blond shrugged off any apprehension he might have been feeling and was about to lean down to kiss Adam again when he froze.

"What is it?" Adam asked worriedly.

"There's a guy approaching the car."

Adam pushed himself up and glanced in the rear view mirror. "It's the police. Swap seats with me."

"Adam—"

"It's fine. Better they catch me behind the wheel than you!"

Leon could see the sense in that and they were able to make the switch and return the passenger seat to its normal position before the officer arrived at the driver's window.

"Hello again, Joel," Adam said with a grin as he recognised the policeman.

"Mr Larimore," Officer Joel Banks stated curtly. "Do

you have a licence for this vehicle?"

"No," Adam replied calmly. Banks would have checked before approaching them anyway so there was little point in lying.

"Then I'm going to have to ask you to get out of the car. Both of you," Banks frowned as he glanced at Leon. "Who was driving?"

"I was," Adam answered without hesitation.

Banks clearly didn't believe him. "Do you want to think about that? I can smell the alcohol on your breath, Mr Larimore. You may well be over the legal limit for operating this vehicle."

"I probably am," Adam admitted with a sigh. He got out and shut the door after him. Leon had also climbed out of the car although he didn't appear as comfortable with the situation as he came round to join Adam.

"Turn around and place your hands on the side of car. Both of you," Banks ordered. "Do not move. I am armed and I will shoot you if you try to make a run for it."

Even though they both complied Adam contemplated whether he could be quick enough to get back in the car before Banks could get a round off. He might be able to but there was no guarantee that Banks wouldn't shoot Leon instead. Adam wasn't really that concerned with escaping anyway.

"I don't know why you are bothering with all this?" Adam said as Banks started pressing various buttons on the portable breathalyser. "I'll be out by morning!"

"Maybe but your friend won't be. I know he was driving, Mr Larimore."

"Good luck proving it," Adam goaded him. Banks moved further away as he began speaking into his radio. All officers carried portable breathalysers as all offenders were tested as part of standard procedure before being taken to the police station.

"Adam, cool it," Leon murmured.

"It's fine. He'll take us back to the station and we'll get slaps on the wrist," Adam answered confidently.

"Adam," Leon cast a wary glance at Banks before speaking again. "I have Clarity on me."

Drug offences were taken very seriously and as standard procedure Banks would search both of them before taking them back to the station.

"Okay," Adam thought quickly. "When he comes back I'm going to jump him. Get out of here and make sure you dump the drugs in case you're picked up later."

"What if he shoots you?"

"What if he does? I can heal from anything other than a heart or head shot. He won't shoot to kill. He's not that stupid."

"Thanks baby. I owe you one."

They fell silent as Banks re-joined them.

"Stay exactly where you are," he warned Leon before instructing Adam to blow into the top of the breathalyser. The small LCD screen on the side immediately bleeped to confirm what they both already suspected.

"You're well over the limit," Banks said with some satisfaction in his voice. "Adam Victor James Larimore, on behalf of the Government police I am arresting you for breach of section 5, paragraphs 2.5 and 3.9 of the vehicle licensing and operations guidelines. Anything that you say from this point onwards could be used as evidence against you. Do you understand?"

Adam shrugged and, taking the man by surprise, he whirled around and punched him hard enough to cause him to drop the breathalyser onto the concrete. Adam didn't need to look behind to him to know that Leon had made a run for it. Banks' angry shout confirmed that. The officer immediately drew his gun as he scrambled to his feet.

"Get down on the ground!" he shouted as he raised the weapon. Adam didn't hesitate. He lunged forwards and slammed his elbow into Banks' gut. The older man cried out in pain and stumbled backwards. Adam grabbed hold of the gun barrel and attempted to force Banks to release his grip on the weapon. Banks swore angrily as the gun was pulled down. A shot rang out and seconds later Adam felt an excruciating pain in his right thigh. Despite being cavalier about the prospect of being shot the reality hurt much more than he was expecting. He cried out and dropped to the ground. He pressed his hand tightly over the wound to try and staunch the blood flow. Crimson welled up around his fingers and Adam suddenly felt light-headed. Banks took a step back as his furious expression faded into one of almost horror. He was breathing hard as he began talking into his radio.

Adam glanced down at his blood soaked leg and the rapidly growing pool underneath him. There was too much blood…he'd hit the artery Adam thought dizzily as his vision began to fade. He was vaguely aware of Banks' worried yell before everything went black.

CHAPTER SIX

Adam had never been in hospital. Thanks to genetics he couldn't get sick and he'd never had any accidents as a child. It was not an experience that he was keen to have and he inwardly groaned when he woke up to the sterile surroundings and the sight of his father seated in the corner of the private room. Victor was paying more attention to his portable computer than his injured son and it took him a few minutes to notice that Adam was awake. In this time Adam glanced around the room. It was white and sparsely furnished. He was hooked up to a computer, which monitored his heart rate and other vitals. The bed he was lying in was steel-framed and had white sheets and pillows. Adam's left wrist was handcuffed to the bed frame in case he tried to make a run for it. Judging from the pain in his thigh he didn't think that it was likely that he was going anywhere anyway. Not for a few hours at least.

The London Memorial Hospital was the main hospital for the city. Built soon after the war had ended it had a plaque in the reception that was dedicated to those who had lost their lives. The hospital was divided up into two wings. The east wing was for normal citizens and from what Adam had heard it was underfunded and understaffed. Many patients were left waiting hours to be seen and there weren't enough doctors and nurses to adequately care for the patients. In the west wing, where he was, things were different. The west wing only cared for those of affluent backgrounds or who were working for the Government or L.S.A. Patients here got their own room, an individual nurse assigned to them and computer access should they be well enough to use it. They received priority treatment and a better quality of care than those in the east wing.

"What the hell did you think you were doing?" his father demanded when he finally realised that Adam was awake.

Adam scowled; he should have known better than to expect any concern.

"Have you any idea how much trouble you are potentially in? Not to mention stealing Joseph's car. It's been impounded and will cost me quite a substantial sum to get it released."

"What do you want me to say, father? That I'm sorry?" Adam asked wearily.

"That would be a good start," his father huffed in annoyance.

"Well I'm not."

"I didn't think you would be."

Adam shifted on the bed and grunted as a sharp pain shot down his leg. He gingerly moved the covers out of the way with his free hand. He pulled the hospital gown he was wearing up enough to see the white bandage wrapped around his thigh. There was a small spot of blood in the centre of it.

Finally some minor concern registered on Victor's face. "I'll go and get your doctor," he said gruffly before leaving the room. He returned with a pursed-lipped, stern looking woman in her mid-forties. She curtly introduced herself as Doctor Taylor. She checked the computer and then had a look at his wound.

"How are you feeling?" she asked once she had finished.

"I'm in a bit of pain," Adam admitted.

"The bullet struck your femoral artery and as it didn't go all the way through you had to undergo surgery to remove it. That is why you feel some pain. I can give you some morphine for that. You were extremely lucky that your cells started to repair the injury almost immediately after you were shot. If you had been a normal citizen then you would have most likely bled to death before the medics could have reached you. I would think that the wound will have closed completely by tomorrow morning and I would like to keep you in overnight for observation."

"Do I *have* to stay in?" Adam asked. He would rather not if he could avoid it. The idea that he could have died didn't really faze him; why would it when he could heal?

"You will do as the doctor recommends," his father answered before she could.

"I do recommend it," she agreed.

Doctor Taylor checked Adam over quickly and gave him the morphine she had promised. She also suggested that he was left to get some rest before taking her leave. As she was exiting the room another person arrived. Ivan appeared more concerned than Victor and he immediately asked Adam how he was.

"A bit sore, but the morphine should help. What are you doing here, Ivan?"

"I asked him," Adam's father said in annoyance. "We

need to discuss the charges and how best to deal with them."

"We don't need to do this now," Ivan said diplomatically. "It can wait until Adam's feeling better. He won't be taken into custody until he's been discharged from hospital."

"He's not going anywhere apart from Venewood," Victor stated shortly. "I want all charges dropped, Ivan."

Ivan frowned. "It isn't that simple."

"How much will make it that simple?"

"It isn't about money anymore. How many more times, Victor? This is getting seriously out of hand."

"I am still here," Adam snapped. "Don't talk about me like I'm not in the room!"

"We will talk about you however we want," his father shot back. "You are an ungrateful, selfish—"

"Victor!" Ivan cut in hurriedly. "Perhaps we ought to discuss this outside."

"There is nothing to discuss. You will get the charges dropped. I also want the arresting officer sacked. Adam has an important meeting with the L.S.A on Monday, which will have to be postponed if he is not fit enough to attend!"

"Father, please," Adam cut in tiredly.

Victor gave his son a dirty look and stormed out of the room. Adam rolled his eyes, much to Ivan's disapproval.

"I was with Victor when he received the call from the police," Ivan told Adam quietly. "He was worried enough to begin with and when your doctor said that you had to undergo surgery immediately… He was beside himself, Adam."

"I doubt it. He probably wishes I'd died!"

"Of course he doesn't. I know you don't believe it, but Victor does love you. His anger is his way of dealing with his emotions."

"Whatever," Adam dismissed. It didn't matter how much Ivan insisted, Adam didn't believe that his father was that upset over what had happened. He was most likely worried about the bad publicity.

"Can you get the charges dropped this time?" Adam then changed the subject by asking.

"Probably," Ivan admitted, knowing better than to push the previous topic of conversation. "But I won't have Officer Banks fired for doing his job."

"I don't care about that and nor does father, not really. He's just annoyed that he's got to explain to Jeff Ingham why the L.S.A system upgrade has to be put on hold."

"I'll talk to him," Ivan offered kindly. "And I'm going to suggest to him that you come to stay with me and Margaret for a while."

"There's no need for that."

"I think there is. I'm sure Joseph is going to be pretty upset with you. Come and stay with us until things have calmed down at home. It will also give you a chance to consider your future properly."

"You mean working for the L.S.A?"

"I really think you should consider it. It is a great opportunity."

Adam glanced away. After what he had learned the idea of working for that organisation sickened him. Ivan did have a point about Joseph though and considering the mood that his father was in it might be best for Adam to stay away for a while.

"Okay," he agreed finally. "I'll come and stay with you for a bit, but only if you tell father!"

Ivan chuckled. "You don't want to take that bullet?"

"Not considering I've already taken a literal one!"

"All right, I'll speak to him. I'll also go to Venewood and pack some things for you so you can be discharged into my care this afternoon."

"Thanks Ivan. Can you get my computer too?"

Ivan nodded. "There's just one thing. There was another young man with you. Officer Banks said that he fled the scene. It would be easier if we could find him and possibly arrange for some of the charges to fall on him."

"I was alone, Ivan," Adam answered hurriedly. He was glad that his lover had managed to get away, and Adam was determined to make sure that Leon was kept out of this.

"That's not what—"

"I was alone," Adam repeated firmly.

"Okay," Ivan sighed in defeat. "I'll let you get some rest now, Adam, and I'll be back later on this afternoon."

Adam settled back down in bed after Ivan had gone. Thanks to the morphine his thigh didn't hurt as much as it had done when he first awoke. He knew that his healing abilities were playing a role in this also. He slept for a little while and when a nurse came round to check on him he managed to get access to one of the portable computers that were given out to patients. It would seem that his exploits had made it onto the Information Bank's news section this time, however, they were somewhat overshadowed by Eric Rawlins' latest successful mission. He had led a small team to capture some military personnel originating from Scotland who had taken up refuge in London. They were accused of plotting to attack L.S.A facilities in order to steal data and computer programs. Scotland was behind England where technology was concerned and there were often agents who tried to get hold of anything that could potentially help them to catch up.

The defence shield system around London made it impossible for a military assault and on the sides that were landlocked there were security domes manned by lower level L.S.A personnel. Even though an attack on these would also activate the shields, a faked English identity card, wearing someone else's fingerprints and a false English accent was all one needed to circumvent them. The Government probably knew this as well as Adam did, and with relations with the other former members of the United Kingdom being at a low a reconciliation was doubtful.

Adam's gaze lingered for longer on the photo of Eric Rawlins that dominated the news article. He looked uncomfortable, Adam mused to himself. As though he didn't enjoy the spotlight that he had been thrust into. In a way Adam could relate to that. They had both been created for a purpose and nothing more.

At lunchtime a porter came round and brought Adam something to eat. She appeared to be about eighteen and was rather nervous around him. Adam didn't blame her; most people were wary of him thanks to his father's reputation. Adam managed to sit up, however, the handcuff was going to make attempting to eat anything challenging to say the least.

"I don't suppose anyone gave you authorisation to un-cuff me?" Adam asked hopefully.

The brunette shook her head. "No they didn't, I'm sorry, Mr Larimore."

"It's not your fault. I'll try and make do. What is it anyway?" he asked as she set the tray down on his lap. There was what appeared to be a pale grey-blue yoghurt-like substance in a ceramic bowl. This seemed to be the main ‘meal’.

“It’s a protein pack. It contains all the nutrients of a balanced meal,” she explained nervously. “This one is blueberry flavoured.”

Adam dubiously picked up the spoon and took a small mouthful. It was horribly sweet, but left a bitter aftertaste and he hurriedly washed it down with half the water in his glass.

“That’s disgusting,” he told her. “Why are you serving this shit?”

“It’s what we serve to all our patients. Some have trouble keeping food down or eating anything solid so the protein packs are ideal.”

Adam shook his head. “For the amount this is probably costing father I should be served a four course meal and champagne!”

The brunette smiled despite her apprehension. “You can’t drink champagne in a hospital, Mr Larimore!”

Adam chuckled. “Maybe not. I’m sure you can get me something proper to eat can’t you?”

The porter suddenly looked worried. “I don’t know. It’s against hospital protocol. If you were taken ill after eating I would be held responsible.”

“Okay, but I’m not going to eat that so you might as well clear it away now.”

“Are you sure? Dinner isn’t brought round until after 6?”

“I’m sure,” Adam confirmed.

The brunette nodded. She refilled Adam’s glass and kindly left the pitcher too after cleaning up the tray.

It was an hour later before Ivan reappeared. He seemed somewhat stressed as he approached Adam’s bed. He pressed his thumb on the small LCD square in the middle of the handcuffs to release them.

“I take it the charges are sorted?” Adam enquired as he was freed.

“They are,” Ivan confirmed. “And I’ve been to Venewood to collect some of your things. Your father has agreed that it would be best if you stayed with me and Margaret until you’re back at work.”

“That’s two months!” Adam protested.

“It was that or two months jail time. As I said, Adam, it is getting difficult to protect you from the consequences of your actions.”

“Then don’t,” Adam answered shortly.

Ivan was about to reply when Dr Taylor entered the room. She checked Adam over and when she removed his bandage she was pleased to report that his wound had healed sooner than anticipated.

“You may find it a little tender still as there was quite significant muscle and tissue damage,” she said in a tone that clearly said that she did not approve of Adam’s early hospital release. “If you experience any prolonged periods of pain then I suggest you return as an outpatient for another scan. I can arrange a wheelchair to assist you in leaving the hospital.”

“I can walk thanks,” Adam shook his head. “Ivan will help me if I need him to,” he added as an afterthought.

Dr Taylor still appeared doubtful and reiterated twice whilst Adam was reading through his discharge notes on her portable computer that he really ought to reconsider. Adam insisted he was fine and pressed his finger on the square at the bottom of the screen to confirm that he had decided to discharge himself from the hospital.

Once she had gone Ivan handed Adam a small silver

cloth bag which contained some clothes. The older man then left the room to give Adam some privacy. The pair of corded grey trousers and white long-sleeved shirt weren't from Adam's wardrobe and were a bit loose on him. He said as much when Ivan returned a few minutes later.

"All of your trousers are too snugly fit," he said in explanation. "I thought they'd probably aggravate your injury."

"It's healed now. Did you pack any of my own clothes?"

Ivan chuckled and shook his head. "Heaven forbid you dress sensibly, Adam. Yes I have. They are in my car."

"What about the clothes I was wearing last night?"

"The medics had to cut your trousers to treat your wound. I believe they have been disposed of."

"What about my top?"

Ivan sighed in exasperation. "Does it really matter, Adam? You have enough outfits to clothe half the city."

"They were made to order," Adam responded in annoyance. The loss of the trousers was fair enough. Even if the medics hadn't cut them, bloodstains were a pain to remove, but the top was a needless waste.

"I'm sure you'll survive without them," Ivan seemed irritated and so Adam decided to let it go.

"Yeah you're right," he replied as he tentatively tried to stand up.

"Are you sure you don't want a nurse to bring you a wheelchair?" Ivan asked when Adam was forced to grab hold of the headboard to steady himself.

"I'm fine," he insisted. Getting changed had been relatively straightforward but walking was another matter. As the doctor had said, even though on the surface his wound had healed he could still feel it twinge as he moved. Determined not to be beaten, Adam merely gritted his teeth and gave Ivan a small smile as he managed to take a couple of steps forward.

The older man shook his head and offered Adam his arm.

"Thanks," Adam murmured as he took it and allowed Ivan to lead him out of the room. A few people stopped to stare at them as they walked towards the exit. Evidently his exploits had been noticed despite the L.S.A's attempt to steal the spotlight.

Walking was more painful than Adam let on and he was glad when they reached Ivan's car. He grimaced slightly as he got into the passenger side and this did not go unnoticed.

"I don't want to echo your father, but what were you thinking?" Ivan asked quietly as he started the engine.

"I think it's obvious that I wasn't thinking," Adam answered in annoyance. The last thing he wanted was another lecture.

"For a smart young man you sometimes behave so foolishly."

"How do you want me to behave?" Adam snapped. Ivan's comment had really got to him. How else could he react when all his father did was criticise him? He told his godfather as much.

"Look," Ivan said patiently. "I understand why you feel the need to lash out, but all you're doing is pushing your father further away. Why don't you try to work with him?"

"What? Be the perfect son that he so desperately wants?" Adam scoffed.

"Why not?"

"Because..." Adam frowned and stared at the dashboard for a few minutes before continuing. "The only reason I am alive is because he wanted an heir."

"Don't you want to inherit Larimore Systems one day?"

"I don't want to be my father. And that's all he wants."

"Then don't be," Ivan answered. "You are lucky, Adam. You have been born into great wealth and so you have the means to become whoever you want to be. As I said before, Larimore Systems is not all that there is for you. Join the L.S.A and let me be proved right."

Adam stayed silent. He knew better than to mention what he had discovered about the L.S.A. He had to be careful about what he did with this new information. Ivan was to be the Head of the L.S.A. Even if he did know the truth he might not want to do anything about it.

"Adam?" Ivan prompted him. "Are you all right?"

"I'm just thinking about what you said," he lied.

"Good," Ivan nodded in approval.

The drive was completed in more or less silence. Ivan's home was on the top floor of a luxury apartment block in Sector Three. It provided accommodation for senior officials and their families. Ivan lived there with his wife Margaret. The couple were childless.

"I informed Margaret of your stay," Ivan said as they rode the lift to the top floor.

"I expect she was thrilled," Adam answered sarcastically. Margaret Williams was a brunette version of Eleanor Larimore and even vainer. She was slender to the point that it was unhealthy and often worried about her looks. She'd had surgery to reduce lines and rid herself of any blemishes. Yet unlike Eleanor's feelings for Adam's father, it was clear that Margaret adored Ivan. She was less adoring when it came to Adam. She often made snide comments and criticised his actions when Ivan wasn't around.

"She understands that it is for the best," Ivan answered him.

Adam made no comment on this as they stepped out of the lift. Ivan pressed his thumb against the security tile to release the door before ushering Adam inside.

The Williams' home was like most modern era properties. It was furnished in white and chrome and had a clinical feel to it. There were a few digital photo frames depicting images of Ivan and his wife; those were the only personal touches in the entire living space. The bedrooms led off from this. The kitchen was open plan and to the back of the living space. The Williams' also had their own private balcony.

"Adam, darling," Margaret greeted him in a sugary sweet voice. She rose off of the white sofa and enveloped him in an embrace. Adam retained the contact only briefly before gently pulling away. He knew better than to think her attitude towards him had changed. Evidently Ivan had told her to be nice to him.

"Ivan explained what happened. You poor thing, what a terrible business. I've made the spare room up for you. Can I get you anything to eat or drink?"

"No thanks," Adam shook his head. Despite feeling hungry at the hospital his appetite seemed to have vanished during the car ride. "I'm pretty tired. I think I'll go and lie down for a while."

Adam made his escape quickly. The spare room was the one to the left; Adam knew this from staying here before. On a couple of occasions Ivan had picked him up drunk after he'd left the club. Rather than incur his father's wrath Adam had slept it off at his godfather's home.

As the door slid shut he heard some of the conversation between Ivan and his wife.

"Ivan, how long is he going to be staying here?"

"A couple of months, that's all."

"That long?"

"Adam is my godson. What else can I do?"

"And what will Jeff say? He's already concerned about your relationship with Adam as it is!"

"Victor is my best friend."

"And that promotion is your life. It's all you have ever worked for!" she huffed and the voices drew further away. "Victor should have taken that boy in hand years ago. He's a disgrace…"

Adam sighed and stopped listening. He didn't need to hear any more of this.

The spare room wasn't that big and housed a single bed, a set of drawers and a bedside cabinet. Adam took his computer out of the bag that Ivan had packed for him. He sat down on top of the bed and switched it on. He looked back through the files that he had downloaded from the L.S.A's system. It disgusted him how everyone with any power felt that it gave them the right to play God. His father was the same. He assumed that because he'd paid for Adam's creation that he owned his son. He didn't see Adam as a person at all. He was a science project as Joseph had once said. Adam thought back over his stay in the hospital. Even his doctor had viewed him as different. So much was still unknown as not many people were born with as many genetic specifications as he was. Not many could afford it and Adam only knew of one other person who might have an inkling of how he felt.

With this in mind he called up another set of files that he

had downloaded; the personnel files for all L.S.A agents. There were hundreds, but it only took Adam a minute to find the one that he was looking for.

The top level folders contained basic information about Agent Eric Rawlins; such as age, height, weight, blood type and next of kin contact. The second level went into a more detailed medical report and also held some genetic information. The specification/job description reminded Adam of the one that he had found for himself on his father's computer. Reading on Adam was shocked when his gaze fell on two names that he was not expecting. He had seen the occasional PR shot of Eric with Yvonne Rawlins, the woman who had given birth to him. According to this they weren't genetically related. The information Adam was reading was marked 'classified' and he doubted that even Eric was aware of the identity of his biological parents. The L.S.A were unlikely to reveal this information unless they had a reason to do so.

The more he read the more felt sorry for the poor guy. Even his relationship was a lie according to this file. His life was even worse than Adam's. At least Adam had his freedom, most of the time anyway. Eric had been engineered purely as the L.S.A's PR boy yet he was under the illusion that he really was a superhero fighting to defend the city. In reality he was fighting to protect the L.S.A and Government's interests, which were completely different to what was best for the people. They'd even gone as far as to plant a microchip in his head that dealt him extreme pain if he ever attempted to defy them.

Adam was soon fully engrossed in what he was reading and the afternoon went by quicker than he thought it would.

Finally Ivan entering the bedroom drew Adam's attention from his computer.

"How are you feeling?" Ivan asked.

"Still a bit sore. Much better than I was though."

"Good. Margaret has prepared a light tea for us." The tone in his voice indicated that Adam couldn't request to eat in his room. He reluctantly put his computer away in his bag.

"What were you reading about?" Ivan asked casually as they went back into the living room.

"Just the news," Adam replied as a hologram card on the coffee table bearing the L.S.A logo caught his eye. He picked it up and activated it. It was an invitation to Jeff Ingham's forty years of Government service party in three months' time. Adam recalled seeing his father with a similar invitation. It was plus one and Eleanor would most likely accompany her husband.

"Will everyone from the L.S.A be going to this?" he asked.

"I would imagine so. It is an important event."

Adam nodded to himself as a half-plan began to form in his mind. He couldn't just forget about what he had learned and he couldn't just leak the information either. He would be arrested and the Government would most likely deny it. Adam wasn't exactly popular with anyone and he wouldn't be believed. He needed someone whom the public would believe without question. Eric Rawlins was that person. The public loved him and this also protected him from much of the backlash. The truth would be revealed and the discredited Government would have to do away with the L.S.A completely and make significant changes. And that was where Adam could help them. As much as Adam was disgusted by the L.S.A he had also thought about how their downfall could benefit him. He already had designs and ideas for the technology to assist a different kind of world. They would need his input and expertise. He would finally achieve something for himself and away from the influence of his father. He would no longer need Larimore Systems or his father's name. He would be free of him.

"I want an invitation to this," Adam requested thoughtfully as he handed Ivan the hologram card. Eric Rawlins was bound to be there and this would be the perfect opportunity to make his acquaintance.

"I didn't think you enjoyed these social occasions?" Ivan asked doubtfully, making reference to Adam failing to attend any that he had received previous invitations to.

"I've been thinking a lot about what you said. I thought perhaps I could go to this and network a bit. You know, see the human face of the L.S.A."

Ivan clearly took this as a sign that Adam was seriously contemplating his offer and nodded in agreement. "I can arrange that, but on one condition. You keep yourself out of trouble until then. No more reckless behaviour, late nights or drinking. I certainly don't want to have to bail you out of a police cell again."

"Okay," Adam agreed. He couldn't deny it was going to be difficult to keep himself out of all trouble until the night of the party, but if that was what it took then he would do it.

"Good lad," Ivan replied.

CHAPTER SEVEN

Adam took a sip from the glass of expensive red wine that he'd been given as he glanced around the room. The party in Jeff Ingham's honour was just as dull and difficult to endure as Adam had imagined it would be. Over the last few months he had kept his end of his bargain with Ivan and had managed to more or less stay out of trouble. This hadn't gone unnoticed by his father either although his only comment had been he was 'glad that Adam had seen sense at last and was starting to grow up and take a bit of responsibility'. Refraining from arguing with his father or Joseph had been the hardest part and Adam was looking forward to the night ending so that he did not have to continue to bite his tongue at every snide remark that was made to him.

Joseph was not present tonight. It was too prestigious an occasion for an office junior to be invited to. Eleanor was also absent. She had come down with one of her migraines a couple of hours before they were due to leave. As he would have been pushed to find a suitable replacement for his plus one at such short notice Victor had begrudgingly asked his son to accompany him. Unknowingly to Victor this actually worked in Adam's favour as he had not yet thought of a satisfactory explanation for his own independent invitation.

Unsurprisingly as soon as they had arrived his father had left him in favour of joining his cronies from Larimore Systems' board of directors and Adam had been forced to fend for himself. He'd been approached by a couple of clients although for the most part he had been ignored. Adam wasn't surprised by this. His trouble with the law and the way he acted was completely at odds with the upper class. They were only polite to him because of his father.

Adam drank the rest of his wine and conveniently enough a waiter hurried over at that precise moment to take the empty glass and replace it with another full one. Adam looked around the luxury second floor conference room in the Waterview Gardens complex that overlooked the Thames in Sector Three. Located close to the L.S.A headquarters it was the ideal venue for an event such as this.

The conference room was a spacious area with glass windows on the front that opened out into a balcony area. There were several glass-topped tables set up at the back of the room. Two had an assortment of canapés and the third various bottles of wine and spirits. This had all been produced in the factory north of here. The 'rich man's' factory as Leon had referred to it, which existed solely to produce luxuries for events such as this. There had undoubtedly been a priority on food too, and Adam knew that if he went into a store tomorrow in one of the poorer wards he would find that many items, such as bread, would be out of stock. Thinking of Leon, Adam felt some regret that he hadn't seen his lover more than a couple of times since he was shot. He hadn't been able to go to the club and Leon seemed to dislike Adam just turning up at his apartment unannounced for a few hours. Adam had tried to suggest that they spent some time together during the day, but Leon was working extra shifts so it was difficult for him. Adam missed him and not being able to see the blond was another reason why he would be glad when this night came to an end.

To Adam's delight, Officer Joel Banks was one of the policemen overseeing the security of the event. Adam had made sure to catch his eye upon entering the building. The older man had been indifferent towards him, but even so Adam would bet his inheritance that Banks was seething on the inside at the smug smirk that Adam had given him.

The dress code for the event was suits for the men and cocktail dresses for the women; a traditional dress etiquette that dated to the time before the Great Tsunamis. Adam hated formal wear and, much to his father's horror, he had chosen to wear a pair of tight leather trousers and a silk white shirt. His long hair was loose and he'd woven several braids into each side. To Adam's surprise his father had decided not to insist that he change. Victor had been rather quiet on the drive. Adam figured that he had probably managed to do something to upset him and his father would inform him of it when the evening was over. No one had commented on Adam's clothes anyway. Most of them wouldn't dare and those that would had most likely decided that it would cause Victor more embarrassment if they did.

Adam moved back towards the canapé table. He had seen Eric Rawlins a couple of times, however, with Bex Vixen hanging onto his arm almost constantly the opportunity for

Adam to introduce himself hadn't yet presented itself.

"Adam?" he glanced up when he heard his name being called. Adam saw Ivan walking towards him. With him was another man. Adam looked the newcomer up and down. He was a short man in his late forties or early fifties with either badly thinning light brown hair or a poorly made toupee. He wore a pair of black-framed glasses and his suit was a size too big for him, indicating that he'd either purchased it in a hurry or he had borrowed it from someone else. He had some lines on his face that crinkled when he smiled. Adam held the man's gaze, not really knowing what to make of the familiarity that the man displayed upon seeing him. Adam was certain he had never met him before.

"Are you enjoying the evening?" Ivan asked as his gaze flitted briefly to the now half empty glass in Adam's hand.

"There's free alcohol, what could be better?" Adam answered with a grin as he deliberately took another sip of his wine.

Ivan frowned whilst the man at his side chose to laugh almost ridiculously loud. It wasn't *that* funny, Adam scoffed.

"Adam, this is George Southerly. He's one of the lead geneticists at the London Hospital of Advanced Genetic Sciences," Ivan finally introduced the man.

He grinned again and immediately held out a hand. His palm was rather clammy and he held onto Adam's hand for longer than was proper decorum. In the end Adam had to pull away. His name sounded somewhat familiar. Maybe Adam *did* know him.

"I'm very pleased to meet you," Southerly said enthusiastically. "Ivan's told me so much about you."

"Really?" Adam shot Ivan a questioning glance. "Only

the good I hope!"

Again the man cackled in amusement at Adam's comment. "He has mentioned your unfortunate exploits yes. I understand that you were hospitalised recently"

"It wasn't serious," Adam answered dismissively. "I was released the next day."

"Yes. I saw your notes," Southerly nodded.

"You saw my notes?" Adam asked with some indignation. They were supposed to be confidential.

"Sorry," Southerly now appeared embarrassed. "I rather assumed you'd know me by name at least. I was the geneticist who met with your father twenty years ago. I was responsible for your creation. As part of the contract with Mr Larimore I am privy to your medical notes if you're hospitalised."

Adam felt his hand holding the glass tighten to the point that he was surprised it didn't crack. Contract? So was he just a project to this asshole?

"I wasn't aware that my doctor-patient confidentiality could be violated simply because of a contract that my father made and one that I didn't agree to," Adam shot back testily.

"George, perhaps—" Ivan began to intervene, but Southerly cut him off.

"I must apologise, Adam. I had not realised that you didn't know. It is standard practice with babies who had as many genetic manipulations as you. It is especially important in your case as you are a perfectly genetically engineered human. Wouldn't you agree?"

Adam struggled to disguise his outrage at being yet again referred to as a science project rather than a human being. "So I'm your perfect creation am I?"

Southerly failed to detect the displeasure in Adam's voice

and continued. “You defined my career. At the time your creation was one of the most complex. Of course, there is still so much more to learn from studying you, and others like you.”

“I’m pleased to hear I had such an impact,” Adam answered stiffly. As much as he wanted to have a go at the bastard, if he caused a scene he would most likely be thrown out and he couldn’t risk this when he hadn’t been able to speak to Eric Rawlins yet. “Now, if you’ll excuse me,” as he tried to get away Southerly stepped into his path in a bid to stop him.

“Perhaps we could continue our discussion in private?” he suggested. His uncomfortable tone was now indicating that he was aware that he had annoyed Adam. “Reading your notes only tells me so much and I would very much appreciate the opportunity to discuss the possibility of me conducting a few simple tests of your healing abilities. It would greatly assist my future research and also the creation of others like yourself.”

“That is completely out of the question,” Adam shot back immediately. He turned and hurried away before the geneticist could protest further. How dare Southerly talk to him like that? Adam shook as he struggled to contain his upset. Everyone just saw him that way; as an experiment. He wasn’t real to anyone here.

“Adam!” Ivan hurried after him and gently caught his arm. “I’m sorry. I didn’t realise Southerly was going to speak so out of term. If I had then I would never have introduced you.”

“He talked about me like I was some kind of experiment, Ivan!” Adam said shrilly, his voice trembling with emotion. “Is that all I am to everyone?”

"No," Ivan shook his head. "Adam, you've had too much to drink and it's making you overreact. Come on let's get something to eat," he nodded towards the tables at the back of the room.

"Okay," Adam drew a deep breath. He didn't think he was overreacting at all.

Adam was silent for a moment as he struggled to calm himself. If he caused a scene then he wouldn't be able to speak to Eric and he'd endured so much to get to this night.

Ivan appeared satisfied that a disaster had been averted and started to lead the way towards the table.

"So how did it go with the L.S.A this week?" he asked casually. Thanks to Adam's hospitalisation and then subsequent delays from the L.S.A themselves Adam had only just completed upgrading their computer systems and training the staff.

"Fine," Adam answered. "The upgrade caused only a few minor disruptions to non-essential services."

"That's good. Was Mr Ingham pleased with it?"

"Of course. The new system is state-of-the-art."

"Excellent!" Ivan clapped a hand on Adam's shoulder. "I know you're still reluctant, but you would be an asset to—" he broke off when he caught sight of one of his officers in the force beckoning him.

"I'll be back in a moment," he said to Adam before hurrying across the room towards the other man. Seconds later Adam heard laughter rising up from their discussion. So much for a moment, he thought. Adam handed his glass back to a passing waiter before continuing to make his way slowly towards the canapé tables. He'd never really cared much for this kind of finger food, however, the chocolate fountain dessert that had been wheeled in about fifteen minutes ago was another story. Starting a dessert, especially something clearly marked as a centrepiece, before the savoury canapés had been cleared away was considered by most of the upper class as a major breach in etiquette. Adam, however, couldn't care less about manners. The chocolate fountain had been placed at the side of the room nearest to the balcony. As most of the guests were in groups talking in the middle of the room or congregating around the canapés Adam was pretty confident that he could get away with it.

He casually made his way over to the mountainous dessert and selected a fresh strawberry from the silver platter of fruit that decorated the edges. He dipped it under the dark chocolate waterfall and then took a bite. As he did so he suddenly became aware of someone watching him.

Adam's approach meant that his back was to the room itself and he was facing the balcony. As he glanced up his gaze met that of the man watching him.

Eric Rawlins stood outside. He was leaning against the balcony rail facing the glass windows back into the room. He was wearing the desired formal attire of the evening although he had taken his jacket off and this was folded over one arm. As Adam held his gaze he felt a curious jolt of emotion that he hadn't experienced before. He likened it to attraction, but it felt more than that somehow. He couldn't really describe it and the feeling was making him uncomfortable. Adam swallowed hard and deliberately looked away. However, he could still feel Eric's eyes on him.

Adam forced himself to finish the strawberry that was still clutched tightly between his thumb and forefinger before raising his head to stare at Eric again. The older man was still looking at him. His expression showed some mild horror at the lack of Adam's manners where the dessert was concerned. Adam smiled, and it was momentarily a genuine one, before his usual confident smirk replaced it. Judging from the hero's startled expression, Eric clearly didn't know how to react. If he had any other topic to discuss then this would have been a rather enjoyable conversation Adam thought regrettably as he started to walk towards the balcony doors. He was almost there when he felt a hand on his shoulder.

"Adam," his father said curtly as Adam turned around. "We're leaving."

Adam brushed his father's hand away and shook his head. "No. We've only just arrived."

"We're leaving," Victor repeated firmly. "*Now.*"

"No. I'm not—"

"Adam," his father reached out and took hold of his arm, jerking Adam away from the balcony doors. "Please."

Adam hesitated as he detected a slight quiver to his father's voice. The grip on Adam's arm was painful though unintentional. The older man seemed agitated, worried almost.

"Victor?" Ivan asked as he crossed the room. He had seen what was going on and feared that there was about to be another altercation between father and son. "Is everything okay?"

"Fine thank you, Ivan. We were just leaving."

"In a few minutes," Adam corrected his father as he eased himself from the older man's grasp. "I just need to…" he trailed off as he glanced outside. Bex Vixen had now joined Eric on the balcony. The hero had his back to Adam and seemed absorbed in the conversation. Adam mentally cursed his father. Now he would have to create another opportunity to speak to Eric.

"Never mind," he sighed. "Let's go. Bye, Ivan."

"Goodnight Adam, Victor."

Adam trailed after his father as they made their way to the door, down the stairs and then out of the building. He felt fed up and angry that after all he had done to get to tonight his father had ruined everything. As usual.

"I don't see why you had to drag me away from the party too," he couldn't help but snipe as they made their way out onto the street.

"I was not going to leave you there," his father answered stiffly. "Who knows what you might have done to embarrass me in my absence."

Adam rolled his eyes as they reached Joseph's car that they had borrowed for the evening. "What trouble could I have caused in there?"

"You would have found some way," Victor shot back as he pressed his thumb against the pad to unlock the car doors. "Now can I trust you to get us both home in one piece?"

"You want me to drive?" Adam asked in surprise. "As we've recently established, I do not have a licence."

"Consider it a reward for your better behaviour," his father said as he climbed into the passenger seat. Adam frowned. There was certainly more to it than that, but he wasn't going to turn the opportunity down. He slid into the driver's seat and started the engine. Adam smirked at the tense look on Victor's face as he pulled the car away from the roadside, the speed monitor steadily climbing as they left Waterview Gardens behind. He switched the operation to manual and placed his hands on the steering wheel.

"Adam," Victor said warningly. "Slow down."

The younger man sighed and grudgingly heeded the request. Adam glanced at his father and frowned. Victor's usually tan complexion was pale and there was some sweat beading on his forehead.

"Father, are you well?" Adam asked worriedly. This simple concern seemed to only ignite fury in the older man.

"What do you think? I've been having to run Larimore Systems and do the majority of your work since your suspension. I am fucking exhausted, Adam."

"You didn't have to suspend me."

"I had no choice."

"What do you mean?"

"The board is very concerned about your behaviour and have demanded that I take you in hand. Luckily for you they have not demanded your dismissal as you bring in so much money for the company. However, that does not mean that I cannot discipline you or suspend you when your behaviour is unacceptable."

"Discipline me?" Adam echoed disdainfully. "I'm *nineteen*, father."

"You don't act it. You are a constant disappointment to me, a failure. I had hoped that thanks to science I could have the heir that I always wanted. A perfect son to pass on the mantle and continue the Larimore family business. But instead I ended up with you."

Adam cast a glance at his father again. "Is that really what you think of me?" he asked quietly.

"I always wanted a son," Victor admitted grudgingly without answering the question.

Momentarily Adam's anger faded. It was replaced by a brief hope that perhaps it wasn't too late, that they could find a way to mend their relationship. Adam would be lying if he said that he didn't want to. He remembered a few times when he was a child and he would accompany his father on business trips. A trip to Bournemouth stood out in his mind more than most. Whilst his father was conducting business in the city he had taken a walk along the beach. There had been a few older kids there skipping stones across the water. Adam had been laughed at when his attempts at it only resulted in the stones sinking after one bounce. It had been his father who had taught him the technique. He had returned from his meeting early and observed Adam's efforts. It was one of the few happy memories Adam had of the two of them.

"Father…I hate things being like this between us, don't you?"

"You caused all of this, Adam."

Adam shook his head. "You pushed me away. Ever since I found out about my creation you've kept me at arm's length. You said you wanted a son, but you treat me more like a failed project."

"You are a failure," Victor snapped.

"You…you don't love me then?"

"Love you?" his father questioned almost scornfully. "How could anyone love a son like you?"

Adam's grip on the steering wheel tightened. He felt tears prickling his eyes and he did his best to force them away. The last thing Adam wanted was his father to see how much his cruel words had affected him. He took a deep breath and forced himself to focus on the road in front of him. He wanted to retort, but what was the point? He had tried to be honest about what he was feeling and once again his father had pushed him away. Yet as Adam drove past several high-rise apartment blocks a disturbing notion crossed his mind. Even though cars today were more sturdily built they could not withstand a sudden impact with the side of a building. All he had to do was jerk the wheel to the left and he would be free. His father had no healing abilities. He would die and his fortune and Larimore Systems would pass to Adam. A tragic end to Victor Larimore's legacy, that's all anyone would think. An accident. A terrible accident.

Adam inhaled sharply, dragging himself from his thoughts as the horror of what he had just contemplated slammed into him. This was his father. Not moments before he had been reaching out, wanting to rebuild their relationship. How could he think such terrible things mere seconds later? Despite what his father said or did, Adam could never want him dead. *What was all this cruelty and all this rejection turning him into?*

Impulsively he slammed on the brakes, sending the car into a violent halt that jolted them both forward.

"Adam?" Victor demanded, the hint of a temper entering his voice. "What are you doing?"

"You can fucking drive yourself home," Adam hissed as he opened the door.

"Adam!" Victor called furiously after him. "Get back here right now. Adam!"

Adam ignored him as he began walking briskly in the direction of the river, leaving his father's shouts far behind him.

CHAPTER EIGHT

Adam sighed to himself as he switched on his computer and loaded the Information Bank. It had been a week since the party and so far he had been unable to find another opportunity to meet Eric Rawlins. Adam grit his teeth in frustration as he thought back over that night. Albeit unintentionally his father had ruined everything.

After he had eventually gone back home Adam had received a scolding from Eleanor for abandoning Victor. Joseph had gone to 'rescue' him and had wasted no time in telling everyone who would listen how Adam had left his unwell father on the roadside. Overdoing things at work was hardly a serious medical condition Adam had scoffed dismissively. It was just another thing that his father could use to make Adam look like the villain.

How could anyone love a son like you?

His words still hurt and Adam knew that they always would. Despite everything he had hoped that some part of Victor cared for his son. Now that hope was dead, and Adam knew it was time to focus on more important things; exposing the L.S.A and Government for what they truly were.

To do that he needed Eric. He had casually asked Ivan if there was a possibility that he could meet the hero, but Ivan had seemed reluctant to help him. He had still been pushing Adam for his decision and Adam had been forced to admit that he had no intention of joining the L.S.A. Ivan's response to this had been one of disappointment. He clearly thought that Adam was making a mistake.

There had to be another way in Adam thought to himself as he consulted his computer. It was ironic how the criminals and terrorists seemed to have an easier time meeting Eric Rawlins in person that London's citizens he mused as he read over the latest news from the L.S.A. Eric and his 'girlfriend' had just foiled another plot by Scottish militants. Maybe that was it, Adam thought to himself. With his computer skills he could certainly fake a security risk or something along those lines that in reality was completely harmless, but with any luck the L.S.A would perceive it a significant enough threat to send their star agent to defend the city. It would have to be a location where Adam could get Eric alone long enough to at least tell him some of what was going on. Adam thought over this problem for several minutes before the answer came to him. Larimore Systems had just installed a new defence program at each of the four nuclear power plants. This defence system could be overridden by a small backdoor program that Adam had developed. With a few modifications he could amend it to allow him access to one of the plants and then trigger a security alert. Security protocols would mean that the building was isolated once the defence system had been activated, which Adam would not do until Eric came to investigate.

Adam decided to make a start on the modifications tonight and he had just begun when the call symbol at the bottom of his computer screen started to flash.

"Hey, Adam," Leon greeted him as Adam pressed the phone icon to connect the video call. "Are you busy tonight?"

Adam hesitated. He felt torn between his desire to see his lover and working on his program.

"I've got some work to do," he finally answered regretfully.

"That's a real shame," Leon commented in response to this. "Seeing as I came out of my way to see you."

"You're here?" Adam asked in surprise. He paid attention to the background on the screen for the first time and recognised the apartment block across the street from Venewood.

"Yeah," Leon grinned. "So you coming out or not?"

"I really ought to get my work finished, Leon."

"Adam," Leon's voice definitely had a disappointed edge to it. "I really want to see you. Surely what you're doing will keep for a few hours?"

Adam hesitated; he had not seen that look before. The blond seemed genuinely upset. Maybe he did have deeper feelings for Adam than he wanted to admit to?

"Yeah it can," Adam decided. Exposing the L.S.A was important, but so was Leon.

He shut down his computer and put it on his bedside cabinet before hurrying downstairs.

When Adam stepped outside he found that Leon had moved and was standing next to the front door.

"Hi," he grinned before pulling Adam into a kiss. Even

though his boldness took Adam a little by surprise he didn't pull away. He felt arms around him and then suddenly he was turned and pushed back against the doorframe.

"Do you wanna go to the club?" Leon murmured against Adam's ear. "Or shall we just go back to mine?"

"We could just stay at Venewood," Adam suggested. He was barely able to conceal his delight that Leon had clearly missed him and again that hope that they could have more than a casual relationship sparked within him. Any misgivings that Adam had about putting his L.S.A plan on hold were rapidly fading.

However, Leon's reaction to Adam's suggestion was one of apprehension. "What about your father?"

"He's not here. We have the whole house to ourselves," Adam assured him.

"So," Leon commented when Adam unlocked the door and stepped aside so that he could enter. "This is how the rich minority live."

Adam shrugged as he pressed the tile on the wall to close the door behind them. "A golden cage is still a cage no matter what it's worth."

Leon sniggered as he glanced around at the marble and wooden furnishings. "Are you kidding? This is fucking amazing!"

Adam grinned and forced himself to dismiss his words. "Yeah I'm kidding. This place is a palace. Would you like a guided tour?"

The blond's expression turned from smug to hesitant. "You're sure this is okay, right?"

"Why wouldn't it be?"

"We could just go back to mine."

Adam sighed impatiently and took hold of Leon's hand. He pulled the blond in the direction of the stairs. "Come on."

"I've missed you," Leon murmured as they made the ascent. "It's been kind of lonely without you around."

Adam kept his back to his lover so that Leon couldn't see the pleased smile on his face. As they reached the top of the stairs he felt Leon's arms around him. Adam was turned around and then pushed back against the wall as Leon kissed him. Adam tried to slow the pace and kept his response tamed compared to the fierce embrace of Leon's that left him breathless.

"Leon," Adam reluctantly parted them. "Can we talk first?"

"What about?"

Adam didn't often feel apprehensive, however, the almost irritated way that Leon was looking at him was making him nervous. "I…I really like you," he admitted softly.

"I like you too," Leon replied almost dismissively as he pulled Adam away from the wall and the down the corridor. "Which room is yours?"

"The third one."

The hint of resignation in Adam's voice was lost on his lover and so he forced any misgivings he had aside. They hadn't seen each other in a while and there would be time to talk properly later Adam told himself. After all they had all night.

"Are you sure your father isn't home?" Leon sought to clarify as he kissed Adam. This time the younger man allowed himself to fully give into the embrace. He kissed Leon back with just as much enthusiasm. Adam fisted a hand in blond locks to roughly jerk them apart long enough so that he could smirk at Leon's concern and vocalise a reply.

"He's gone into the city with his wife. I imagine they will be out for hours."

Leon's hesitancy faded as Adam leaned forward to kiss him again. He wrapped one arm around Adam's waist whilst his free hand felt for the tile that would release the door. After several seconds of searching he found it and practically shoved Adam over the threshold as the door slid open. Adam felt the backs of his legs hit the foot of his bed and then Leon was pushing him down onto it. The blond's kisses had now become even more demanding. He straddled Adam's waist, nipping Adam's lower lip hard enough to break the skin before drawing back. He gripped the hem of Adam's white tank top and Adam barely had time to raise his arms over his head as Leon pulled the garment off of him. He threw it aside before leaning down to kiss Adam again. Leon momentarily rested his left hand against the side of Adam's face. His fingers gently caressed Adam's cheek before they slid up into his dark hair and pulled Adam's head to the side.

"Fucking tease," Adam groaned as he felt lips kissing a path down his throat.

"You know you love it really," Leon answered breathlessly. Adam nodded quickly. At this point he was too bothered by Leon's ministrations to summon a verbal response. Leon drew back long enough to undo Adam's jeans. He pulled them, and his underwear, down Adam's legs. Adam had to kick them off as Leon left them at his ankles in favour of removing his own clothing.

"Adam?" Adam froze, shocked out of the moment when he suddenly heard his father's voice on the stairs. Leon drew back, his expression one of fright as they both heard Victor approaching the room.

"Fuck!" Adam cursed as he shoved Leon aside. Much to his dismay he realised that they had left the door open. Adam was trembling as he grabbed the edge of the duvet, barely managing to cover himself as his father appeared in the doorway.

"Adam, before you left the office yesterday did you—" Victor trailed off as he took in the scene before him. Adam's hands gripped the duvet so tightly that his knuckles whitened. As father and son stared at each other Victor's expression went under a slow metamorphosis. Shock slowly melted into fury as his pale face reddened and his hands began to shake.

"Get out," Victor directed this command at Leon although his gaze did not leave his son's face. Adam swallowed hard when the blond failed to make a move. If Leon didn't leave then it would only make matters worse. Adam didn't know what his father was going to do to him, but he didn't want Leon getting caught in the middle of it.

He shook his head at his lover, feeling tears welling up in his eyes as Leon cast him a sympathetic look. He retrieved his clothes from the floor and fled before Victor could change his mind.

"Put your clothes back on," his father then demanded in a voice that was cold and yet calm. For now. Adam had borne the brunt of his father's temper on too many occasions to think that he could reason with him. Victor would never understand and Adam knew that it was futile in trying to get him to listen. More tears blurred his vision as he shakily did as he was told. All the while his father stood over him; his fury barely concealed beneath that cool mask.

Adam drew a deep breath when the silence dragged on for

longer than he could stand. He knew what was coming and he just wanted it to be over with. "Father, I'm—"

Despite the anticipation, the blow that his father dealt him still caught Adam by surprise. He fell back into the wall, wincing at the vicious pain that was his father's fist connecting with his cheek. He bowed his head to disguise both his discomfort and the tears that were fast threatening to fall.

"Despite many disappointments I still had hope for you," his father snarled furiously. "The drinking, the fighting and vandalising of Government property…I told myself that perhaps this was a phase that you were going through and that you'd grow out of it in time but this…disappointment is much too mild a word to describe how I am feeling right now. I am ashamed and disgusted by what I've witnessed tonight."

"I can't help who I am," Adam mumbled tearfully. The look on Victor's face; the loathing, the disappointment…this hurt far more than words ever could. Despite everything a small part of Adam had hoped that one day his father might treat him more kindly or even give him some indication that he felt something for Adam. This hope was now well and truly dead. All Victor cared about was his empire.

"This…this isn't who you are. Do you really think I would have had you engineered like this? One day you are supposed to get married and continue the family line. This is nothing more than a pathetic attempt to defy me and it has to stop. Now."

"And if I don't?" Adam ventured softly, feeling a flickering of anger rising to the surface. For all of his life his father had told him what a disappointment he was. At first Adam had tried so hard to make him proud, but trying to be the perfect son that Victor had wanted wasn't enough. His rebellion came from his anger and this anger was now overcoming Adam's shock and fear. He glared defiantly at his father as Victor's expression changed from furious to determined. He did not speak as he lunged forwards and seized Adam roughly by the arm.

Initially Adam was too stunned to put up any resistance as he was hauled from the room. Then as they reached the stairs the pain of his father's grasp penetrated through his shock and Adam began to struggle.

"Father, you're hurting me," he pleaded. He was being dragged down the stairs until all of a sudden Victor released his grip and pushed Adam roughly forward. Adam cried out as he tripped. Thankfully he was only on the last couple of steps but even so the impact still hurt. Pain shot through his shoulder and yet this barely registered when Adam suddenly felt a sharp pull on his hair. He stumbled to his feet and vaguely heard Eleanor's worried voice in the background as he was hauled towards the front door.

"Father. Please…you're hurting me," he continued to beg. However, his pleas only served to infuriate his father further. He was pushed forcibly against the wall and a further blow followed. Adam tasted blood in his mouth and for the first time he felt truly afraid. His father's temper was out of control. The darkened look in the older man's eyes confirmed this. Adam had got into enough fights to be able to defend himself, but this was different. He found that he couldn't move. He couldn't raise a hand to protect himself. The utter powerlessness that he felt rocked him to the core. All he could do was withstand the assault until it was over. Adam gasped as his father's fist slammed into his stomach. He was still doubled over in pain when his felt a steel grip on his shoulders that pulled him away from the wall. Victor shoved Adam over the entrance threshold. He fell; propelled by both the ferocity and his own inaction. Adam collapsed onto the pavement sobbing as his father's furious voice cut through the otherwise quiet of the evening.

"Don't even think about coming back tonight. Or tomorrow, or the next night. In fact, don't bother coming back at all!"

Adam vaguely heard the bleep of the door as his father locked it. He could get back in if he really wanted to but Adam knew better than that. The crushing weight of rejection was overwhelming. He entangled hands in his hair, tightening his grip to the point of pain as he cried. His own father couldn't stand him. Was he really such a terrible person? Never before had he experienced such self-doubt. All he had ever wanted was for his father to show him some kind of emotion other than anger and disappointment. He never had and nothing that Adam could do or say would change that.

Eventually he stood and started walking away from Venewood. He didn't really know where he was going. Adam hurried down the street keeping his head down so that passers-by couldn't see his tears. His hands curled into fists as he replayed the confrontation over and over in his mind. There was nothing that he could do to take back what had happened. For the first time he noticed that he wasn't even wearing his shoes or socks. Adam bit his lower lip as with this realisation he started to feel pain as he continued to walk barefoot down the street. Adam briefly contemplated going to Leon's apartment and then dismissed it. He didn't want his lover to see him like this.

This…this isn't who you are. Do you really think I would

have had you engineered like this? One day you are supposed to get married and continue the family line. This is nothing more than a pathetic attempt to defy me and it has to stop. Now

Father. Please...you're hurting me

Round and round in his head all he could hear was his father furious and disappointed words. Nothing Adam had ever done was good enough. He gritted his teeth as he felt anger welling up inside of him once more. He didn't even have his payment card with him. He'd been cast out with no money and nowhere to go.

Wanting to lash out at something – anything – Adam continued to walk down the quiet streets. He wasn't sure where he was heading and at this point he didn't care. Finally Adam found himself standing outside of a convenience kiosk. The kiosk was now closed for the night. Adam stared at the silver and white dome for several minutes. There was a panel on the door, which prevented access. It bleeped in annoyance when Adam activated it. The software was dated, designed by Larimore Systems long before Adam became Development Director, and he knew of several codes that could be used to hack into the system. He inputted one of these now and the door slid open. Adam stepped inside. He paid no attention to the still active security system above his head. He knew the silent alarm would have been tripped and he didn't care.

How could anyone love a son like you?

He wasn't even aware of his fist smashing through the glass of the nearest display until he felt the pain. Automatically Adam pulled his hand back against his chest. His blurred vision stared silently at the crimson welling up rapidly around the shards of glass that were embedded in his skin. Tentatively Adam grasped the largest shard between his shaking fingertips and pulled. He hissed as it grudgingly came free. The blood flow became faster, running down his hand to drip onto the floor. Adam then turned his attention back to the cabinet. He lashed out with his uninjured hand. The blow sent the contents – packets of cereal and several display advertisements – crashing to the floor. The assault was strangely satisfying and without caring for the damage he was inflicting on himself he struck the display on its left. The pain was almost unbearable although it was nothing compared to the agony and desperation that Adam was feeling inside. He prized loose the metal bar affixed to the front of the display. The LCD screen in the centre detailed the prices of each item when the kiosk was open. Adam then moved to the next cabinet and then the next. He brought the metal down hard each time. Glass exploded all around him. Shards struck his face, cutting into his skin and healing almost as soon as it had made contact.

Science experiment…freak…disappointment…

Dimly over the chaos that he was causing Adam became aware of the arrival of the police. He ignored their demands for him to stop. He didn't care what they did to him. An arm encircled his waist and he was dragged forcibly back from the cabinets. Another officer seized the bar and pulled it from Adam's bleeding grasp. Furiously he lashed out. His fist caught the officer behind him in the face. There was shouting and Adam found himself being pushed to the floor. He struck out where he could, kicking and punching, and he was certain he'd landed a few blows at least before his arms were yanked roughly behind his back. Adam felt cold metal handcuffs clamp down over his wrists. He struggled against this briefly, but it was futile. Satisfied that he was subdued, Adam found himself hauled to his feet. The officer standing in front of him seemed to take much delight in informing him that he was under arrest for breaking and entry, criminal damage to property and assaulting police officers. Adam barely acknowledged this. He didn't care what happened to him he realised as he was dragged outside. He didn't care about anything anymore.

CHAPTER NINE

Adam wasn't sure how much time had elapsed since his arrest. He had been detained in the police station in Old Camden for at least a couple of hours. He was locked in a small cell where the only light came in from under the solid metal door. There was a metal bench at the back of the room which he was seated on. Most of his wounds had healed although the deeper cuts to his hands were tender and pain shot through them if he applied pressure to his palms. A medic had tended to him initially, but Adam had refused any further medical attention and pain relief offered to him.

His rage had subsided and now Adam was left feeling empty inside. He had no regrets in smashing the kiosk to hell. However, there was now an uneasy feeling settling in the pit of his stomach. It must have been hours. Even if his father was too angry to be bothered with coming down here then Ivan would have in his place. So far there had been no sign of anyone.

All modern cells were equipped with a green button on the

wall nearest the door. It was used to call for assistance from inside and it could only be activated once. Adam had refrained pushing it until now as there was no guarantee that anyone would come. He could only hope that as he'd been injured when he was brought in they might feel more inclined to answer. He walked over to the door and pressed the button. No buzzer or alarm sounded inside the cell that he could hear. The only way to tell that it had actually rung was that the green light inside of it went out. Adam hovered apprehensively by the door. It was at least five minutes before he heard footsteps approaching his cell. The window in the centre of the door slid back automatically. It revealed the annoyed looking face of one of the arresting officers.

"What do you want?" the blond haired man asked with disinterest.

"I want to make a call," Adam replied. As much as the man's indifference irritated him he knew that if he wasn't polite then his request would be denied.

"That's not going to be possible," the officer flatly refused.

"Wait!" Adam protested as he started to slide the window closed. "I just want to call my father!"

He had expected that this would carry some weight as most people were afraid of Victor. However, the reaction Adam received was unexpected.

"Just a minute. I need to speak to my supervisor."

He disappeared and several minutes went by before Adam heard footsteps returning. Much to his surprise the cell door opened. He took a step back as the open door revealed the blond officer standing with an older man. He was probably a few years younger than Adam's father. He wore the standard Government police uniform except that his had silver epaulettes on the shoulders that indicated rank. He was heavily built and seemed somewhat out of breath as though he had been hurrying. He was unshaven and the bags under his eyes indicated that he had been on duty for well over the standard twelve hour shift.

"I'm Chief Officer Gerrard Howett," he introduced himself. "I'm in charge of this station. I understand that you wish to make a call."

"To my father," Adam nodded. Unease settled in the pit of his stomach as the officers glanced at each other. Howett's detached expression softened and he gestured to the bench at the back of the room.

"Why don't you sit down, Adam. You may leave us, Officer Davies," he added. Officer Davies nodded and left. The door sealed shut behind him.

"What's going on?" Adam asked once they were alone. Howett placed a hand on his back and ushered him in the direction of the aforementioned bench. Adam sighed and slumped down onto it. Much to his surprise the older man sat down beside him.

"What time did you leave your home this evening?"

Adam shrugged. "I don't know."

"And you've had no contact with your family since then?"

"No. What's with the inquisition? I just want to call my father."

"Adam, at approximately 11.16pm there was an emergency call from Venewood. The on-call doctor attended to your father. I am very sorry to have to tell you that despite best efforts he died at the scene."

Adam couldn't breathe. It was as though someone had punched him in the gut. There had to be some kind of terrible mistake. His father couldn't be dead. It just wasn't possible.

"What? I don't understand. He…he was fine when I left. Pretty pissed off actually, but he wasn't unwell," his voice shook dangerously as he spoke and cracked at the end of his sentence. "He was fine…" Adam drew a sharp breath as he fought to regain some of his composure as he stood. This was a battle that he was rapidly losing.

"It was his heart," Howett replied. "He suffered a severe heart attack. I am very sorry, Adam."

"This isn't right. He wouldn't…he couldn't… He wouldn't leave me like that," Adam felt his legs give way and he fell to the tiled floor. He buried his head in his hands as he recalled their argument only hours before. His father had probably died hating him.

Adam knew that he would regret this night forever. Even now his father had won. Adam was left to pick up the shattered pieces that his passing had left behind. He drew a racking breath and fought to disguise a sob as he felt tears wetting his cheeks. He would not grieve for the man he tried telling himself over and over and yet his tears still fell.

"Adam?" he felt Howett kneeling down beside him. "Is there anyone we can contact for you?"

Adam shook his head. "I just want to go home."

"I'm afraid that isn't going to be possible. Do you have a friend that you would like me to call for you?"

"What do you mean it isn't going to be possible?" Adam asked softly as he raised his head to look at the older man.

"In the morning we'll need to interview you and then you will be formally charged."

Adam wiped his eyes. He had assumed that they would let him go. That he'd only have to pay a fine and for all the damages. “Can you call Ivan Williams? He’ll sort all of this out.”

Howett’s understanding expression faded somewhat at Adam’s words though he did not refuse. He left the room briefly. In that time Adam moved back onto the bench. He was shaking and he felt sick. He didn’t want to be in here. Not when he was feeling so much sorrow. Adam just wanted to go home.

He heard footsteps returning sooner than he had anticipated. The cell door did not open, only the small window in the door itself. “Mr Williams is unavailable so I have left a message for him.”

“So I’ve got to stay in here?” Adam asked with some difficulty. The very idea sent curls of panic throughout his body. He *couldn’t* stay in here. Alone with his thoughts and misery and grief…Adam clenched his palms into fists as he felt himself teetering on the edge.

“Despite your circumstances, yes. You’re considered to be a danger to yourself and others. You will be required to undergo a full psychiatric assessment before you can apply for bail.”

“No!” Adam protested vehemently. “You don’t understand. I *can’t* stay in here!”

“Then perhaps you should have considered the consequences of your actions this evening,” Howett advised him.

Adam raced to the door and slammed his hands against the steel. Immediately this set off a series of shooting pains down through his palms. He cried out although the agony did not stop him from striking the door again.

“Let me call Ivan! He’ll speak to me.”

“Mr Williams is unavailable. Now I seriously advise you to calm down.”

“Fuck you!”

“Using language like that will only get you into more trouble,” Howett retorted sternly. “I will have Officer Davies notify your family of your incarceration.”

“Family? What family?” Adam shot back scornfully. Eleanor and Joseph weren’t his family. He had no one. He was alone.

Howett held his gaze for a moment longer before sliding the window shut again. Left alone Adam turned and leaned back against the door as tears welled up in his eyes once more. Slowly his legs gave way until he had slumped down against the steel. He bit down hard on his lower lip to supress a sob. Adam didn’t want to feel grief for the man who had raised him. Victor had not been a father to him. Their relationship had been more akin to employer and employee. He had nothing to grieve for and yet still his tears continued to fall.

***

The next forty-eight hours were a blur to Adam. He had been interviewed yesterday morning and subsequently charged with breaking and entry, damage to property and assaulting two police officers. Adam cared little for the charges and had refused to answer any questions. He also refused to give consent to any kind of evaluation and so he was taken back to his cell where he was told he would be held until further notice. He had asked repeatedly for Ivan and he was told that his godfather was unavailable each time. The refusal was frustrating and Adam found himself cautioned for using abusive language in addition to his charges.

Anger and grief seemed to be a constant war inside of him. Every time he shed a tear for his father he became angry that the man should have such an effect on him. He doubted that Victor would have cared so much if Adam had died. He'd probably have been relieved Adam thought to himself. After all he'd just been a failure and an embarrassment as far as his father was concerned. Victor had not loved his son. But Adam had loved him. He had, deep down. If Adam hadn't cared then he would have left. He could have started up his own company or gone to work for another as soon as he turned eighteen. He hadn't. This wasn't simply because of his inheritance. He had cared that Eleanor had only married his father for his money. He had stayed because he didn't want to see his father hurt. His anger had been blinding him for so long and it had also been protecting him. Without it Adam knew he was vulnerable, and he didn't want to be that person. Not anymore.

He was brought something to eat twice a day, which Adam had refused each time. He felt ill and knew that he'd be sick if he ate anything. The bench was uncomfortable and when he tried to sleep all that happened was that he replayed that night's events over and over in his mind. On the second day of his incarceration, Howett finally returned in the afternoon.

"You have a visitor," he said curtly as the cell door opened. The two officers that were with him escorted Adam back to the interview room. It contained a metal table with a chair on either side. Adam had been expecting to see Ivan and his heart sunk when his visitor turned his head in Adam's direction.

"What do you want?" Adam asked tiredly as he sat down on the free chair. Inwardly he cursed Howett for allowing this.

Adam was well aware that he looked a state; his clothes were torn and bloodied in places, he wasn't wearing shoes and he needed a shower. Adam hated the idea of Joseph seeing him like this. The only comfort was that his stepbrother didn't look great either. He had bags under his eyes and his clothes were rumpled indicating that he'd not yet changed them from the night before.

"I'm here to inform you of arrangements," Joseph answered. He pointedly ignored Adam's tone. He pushed his glasses further up his nose as he continued. "Father's post mortem confirmed that he died of a massive heart attack. His body was released for cremation early this morning. The service will be held this Friday at the old Greenwich and District Memorial centre. All of father's friends and colleagues will be informed. The wake will be at Venewood. Both mother and I were in agreement that it is what he would have wanted."

"So you don't require my input at all?" Adam sneered. "He was my father, remember, and his legacy now passes to me."

"I'm sure his funeral won't cost you too dearly," Joseph replied testily.

"I wasn't talking about the money, but I'm not surprised that you and Eleanor aren't going to spend a penny of the Nichols' life savings."

"I'm not here to argue, Adam. I'm only here because father would want you at the service. Now I have arranged with Chief Officer Howett for you to be released on bail Thursday night. A police escort will bring you back to Venewood. Part of your bail conditions are that you remain there until the funeral."

This did surprise Adam. He had expected that Joseph

would leave him here and he said as much.

Joseph refused to comment and drew the conversation back to the funeral. "I will be giving the eulogy. Mother is in no fit state to speak and we both agreed that it is best that you say as little as possible."

"Whatever," Adam sighed and leaned back in his chair. If he was truthful he didn't want to give a meaningless speech about how close he and his father were and how much he was going to miss the man. However, that didn't mean that he wanted Joseph taking his place.

"Raymond is coming around on Saturday for the reading of the will. I don't expect it will contain anything that we don't already know about," Joseph continued. His tone changed to almost strained at the mentioning of his 'father's' estate. Adam's indifference turned into a smirk, which added to Joseph's annoyance.

"And when it's read I am going to take great pleasure in throwing both you and that harpy mother of yours out of *my* house."

Joseph kept his fists clenched at his sides as he fought back a furious reply. "I only came here to arrange your bail and give you details of the service because, whether I like it or not, you are still father's biological son and we will have to tolerate each other until the funeral is over with. You can rest assured when it is ended *I* will take *great pleasure* in leaving Venewood and Larimore Systems behind. You can sit in that mansion alone with your poisonous thoughts and rot for all I care."

Adam snorted and shook his head. They both knew that Joseph was nothing without Larimore Systems. He was competent at his job at best. Only a good reference from his former employer would open better doors for him and Adam wasn't feeling inclined to give him one or allow anyone else at the company to do so.

"Father emailed me the night he died," Joseph retorted. "He told me that he threw you out. You're lucky I bothered coming at all when it could be said that the stress of your disagreement put further strain on his weakened heart."

"What are you implying?" Adam demanded angrily. "That I caused his heart attack?"

"You certainly didn't help." Joseph stood, clearly not wishing to stay for longer than he had to. "I will see you back at Venewood on Thursday. Try to keep yourself from getting into more trouble, Adam."

"Bye Joseph," Adam called after him in false sincerity. "It was lovely to see you! Remember to spend the next few days packing!"

His stepbrother stalked out of the room and Adam tried to push his comments to the back of his mind. It had occurred to him that their argument had brought on his father's heart attack. Adam didn't want to feel any upset or responsibility for it. He wasn't sure if he could bear it.

"You really are a piece of work aren't you," Howett commented as Adam was escorted back to his cell. "I can see why Mr Williams has washed his hands of you."

"What?" Adam paused by the door. He roughly shrugged off the junior officer's grip on his arm and turned to face Howett. The Chief Officer held up a hand to signal to his men that he didn't perceive a threat.

"What do you mean?" Adam demanded.

"I spoke to Mr Williams yesterday. It is he who has authorised your incarceration and pressing forward with the

the charges against you."

CHAPTER TEN

The Old Greenwich and District Memorial Centre was full to capacity as Adam had expected. He rather doubted that even half of the people here had liked his father, but Victor Larimore had been too prominent a figure for anyone in his social and professional circles to even consider not attending.

The events of the last couple of days had gone by in somewhat of a blur. Adam had been let out on bail on Thursday night and Howett had personally escorted him back to Venewood. He had also assigned two officers to be stationed outside to ensure that Adam didn't try to run away. Escaping was the furthest thing from Adam's mind. He felt exhausted both physically and mentally. Grief and anger had made him too sick at heart to even contemplate taking off. He had barely spoken to Joseph or Eleanor, and he hadn't been allowed any input into today's service. A part of Adam had actually been thankful for this as he doubted that he could have handled it.

Adam stood at the front of the hall next to Joseph. Eleanor

was standing on the other side of her son. She was holding onto his arm and hadn't let go since the service had begun. Despite his dislike for the woman, Adam could see that his father's death had rocked her. She looked as though she had not eaten since it happened. Her expensive custom black mourning dress clung to her frail form. Joseph had commented last night that this would be the first time that Eleanor had left Venewood since Victor died.

Before they had followed the coffin into the impersonal and cold looking square and steel building Adam had been quietly informed that two of Joseph's childhood friends, who were sitting two rows back from them, were under instructions to forcibly remove him if he tried to disrupt the service. Adam had no intention of doing so. Despite his anger towards his father he wouldn't ruin today.

Funerals were simple affairs compared to the ceremonies of the past. The Memorial Centre was one of two this side of the river and was reserved for the rich and those of national importance. The building consisted of the memorial hall where the services took place and the cremation facilities in a separate room at the back. As this centre was strictly for the upper-class it had been furnished with comforting murals on the walls and ceiling depicting the journey of a soul to heaven. Christianity was still the major religion and other faiths could choose to have the centre cater for their individual beliefs. This included the hiding of the murals behind screens if the family of the deceased felt that it was inappropriate to have them on display. Victor had not been particularly religious so it was more social decorum that they were displayed or so Adam presumed. Traditional benches remained for them to sit on. Some services did not play hymns and instead only comforting music produced by the Government's Office of the Bereaved was played. Services were swift and completed within thirty minutes. The vicar would speak first. Family and friends were then invited to speak of the deceased and then Joseph would give his speech before the vicar gave the closing remarks. Cremation was compulsory as there was precious unspoiled land available. Ashes weren't usually returned either unless the family was well off enough to make a special request. Adam didn't know if Joseph had done this.

Marcus Barrow, the Director of Human Resources at Larimore Systems, had just finished his speech. He'd been involved in the company since its formation and recounted how he had worked so closely with Adam's father and spoke fondly of their friendship outside of the workplace. Ivan had spoken before him. His words were mirrored by Marcus and many others. Ivan had refused to even glance in Adam's direction.

It was now Joseph's turn. He gently detached himself from his mother's grasp and stepped up to the small podium. The coffin was directly behind him. Adam avoided looking at the simple wooden box that was his father's last resting place. To do so caused a painful tightening in his throat and he did not want to shed anymore tears for a man who had hated him.

"I'm giving this eulogy on behalf of my mother and stepbrother as they do not feel able to deliver it themselves," Joseph began by saying. "Victor Larimore was my father. Not biologically, but he taught me so much, was there for me whenever I needed him and he loved me as though I was his own son. I've tried my best to put into words what he meant to me, to mother and to Adam."

Eleanor let out the smallest of sobs at this. Her legs gave

way and Adam had to wrap an arm around her to keep her from falling. Momentarily she clung to him, pressing her face into his shoulder before she managed to regain a hold of herself. She pulled back and turned to her father who was standing beside her. The older man gave Adam a cold glance as he comforted his daughter. Adam had only met Graham Nichols a handful of times and the man had never been more than civil towards him.

"So," Joseph continued. "As I'm sure you can tell I haven't written a speech. I've listened to many comforting memories from time spent with my father and I would now like to recall my own. The first was the day that we moved into Venewood. As you all know father had somewhat of a reputation and I was a little unsure of what to expect from him. What I had not expected was that he'd had his housekeeper prepare a wonderful traditional roast dinner for the three of us. I had not quite known what to say to him when he drew me into a hug and told me that outside of the company I was to call him 'father' for as far as he was concerned I was now his son."

Adam recalled that night. He had not been invited to join them. His father had told him that it was a meal just for himself and his new wife. The fact that he had been deliberately excluded hurt even after all these years.

"This is just one example of father's kindness. He was true to his word and treated me as though I was his own son. He was always there to offer me advice and guidance."

Adam silently shook his head. This was utter bullshit. Victor had barely treated Joseph better than he did his biological son. Joseph was given demeaning and junior roles within the company whilst Adam ran his own department, although at home Joseph was favoured over Adam and 'their' father often berated Adam for not being more like Joseph. Professionally speaking straight-laced Joseph showed exactly the right company image and behaved in a way that Victor found agreeable, but it was Adam with the imagination, the intellect and the ability to take Larimore Systems forward. All Joseph would have ever been there was a glorified office boy.

This entire service was a joke. No one knew the real Victor Larimore; the abusive and cruel man who cared very little for anyone unless they were of use to him. Adam couldn't sit through another second of this. So he stood up. Joseph paused, his grey eyes displaying horror as he incorrectly assumed that Adam was about to make a scene. The goons that he had threatened Adam with previously tensed and the bench creaked a warning. Adam shook his head again and merely left the building.

Outside there was a very small garden where people could reflect on times spent with their loved ones. There were white roses, lilies and other white flowers that Adam could not identify. In the centre of the lawn there was a small marble fountain with a bench near to it. Adam went over to this and slumped down. He buried his head in his hands and drew a sharp breath. Then he felt someone else join him.

"Adam?"

"Where the hell have you been?"

His sorrow turned to fury and Ivan flinched at the venom in Adam's voice. He withdrew the hand that had been resting on his godson's back.

"Not here," he requested softly. "This is a place of quiet and reflection, Adam."

"To hell with that," Adam snarled although he did lower his voice. "I've been trying to contact you for days."

"I'm sorry, I've been busy."

"*Busy*?" Adam echoed in disbelief. "I *needed* you, Ivan. You wouldn't return my calls and that bastard Howett said that he won't drop the charges against me because you've given him orders to proceed!"

Ivan sighed. Grief weighed heavy on him also. He appeared tired and somewhat strained by the entire conversation. "I don't know what else to do, Adam. You're out of control. Perhaps a year or so in prison will get through to you where I and your father have clearly failed. I know what you think of Victor, but he did love you, Adam."

Adam swallowed hard as he fought back the tears that were rapidly welling up in his eyes. "Didn't you hear Joseph in there? What he said was all fucking lies. Father *hated* me. The night he died he threw me out!"

"Joseph told me you'd fought," Ivan admitted.

"Do you know why we argued?"

"Joseph did not give me any details."

"He found out I'm gay. I'm sure you can imagine his reaction. He didn't like the idea of the Larimore family line ending with me. He was pretty disgusted too."

"Adam—"

"Our last words were spoken in anger and now…" Adam paused as a sob escaped him. That one slip was enough and before he knew what was happening he felt himself break down. "He's left me feeling like this…I'm so angry…so hate-filled…all the time, Ivan. I don't care who I hurt…myself…others…but I don't want to feel like this anymore. I want to change."

Ivan didn't say anything immediately. The only reaction Adam gained was an arm around his shoulders as he was pulled against the older man. He sobbed harder accepting this comfort as tears fell almost relentlessly down his cheeks. Adam didn't know how much time had passed before he was able to get a hold of himself. Shakily he drew back and wiped his eyes. He felt drained; physically and emotionally.

"I've got to go to Manchester tonight for a few days, but I'll speak to Chief Officer Howett before I leave. You don't need to worry about the charges," Ivan said softly. "But this is your last chance, Adam."

"Thank you," Adam murmured gratefully. "You're always looking out for me, Ivan. You're more of a father to me."

"Adam—"

"I know it's terrible of me to say so, but it's true."

Ivan smiled awkwardly…painfully. Adam sighed and glanced away. His godfather was loyal to his father, even though he knew better than anyone how Victor had treated his son.

"Are you coming back to the house for the wake?" Ivan asked finally.

Adam shook his head. "I don't think so. I'm going to go for a walk. I need to clear my head."

"I'll give everyone your apologies," Ivan said kindly. He gently placed a hand on Adam's shoulder and squeezed slightly. "Look after yourself, Adam."

Adam smiled faintly, but he did not reply. He stood and left the garden just as people started filing out of the centre. No one went after him. Adam knew that Ivan would have deterred anyone who tried.

The city was quite busy at this time of the day and more than a few people stopped him to offer their condolences. Some did this because it was the proper thing to do although a couple seemed sincere. Finally he left the main streets behind. The Thames riverbank had once been a scenic place to walk and take a break from the busy city-life. Now marred by the silver defence shields people could only catch a glimpse of the blue water and imagine what it must have been like before. The defence shields automatically fired on anything that attempted to cross the river.

Adam remained behind them until he reached the New London Bridge. The bridge had its own barrier defence system, which was activated when the L.S.A perceived a threat to the capital. The smaller dome-shaped shields on either side were dormant for now and did not react as Adam stepped onto the bridge. He walked out to the middle and up to the metal rail. After his outburst he felt calmer and more in control than he had been before. In fact Adam realised that he never had been in control before; not really. His father had controlled him. Even his rebellion had been borne out of his desperation to get the man to acknowledge him, to feel something for him. Now he was gone Adam could mourn the relationship they'd never had and even the man himself. Adam wasn't so heartless that he couldn't feel anything for his father. Adam mused that perhaps it was selfish to feel so much relief, but this was a new beginning for him. A chance to turn things around as he had said to Ivan.

Adam sighed to himself and turned so that he was looking back towards the city as thoughts of the L.S.A and the lie that was being told came to the forefront of his mind. It was time to take Larimore Systems in a new direction. He might not be able to tell the country the truth and reveal the true natures of those who claimed to have its best interests at heart, but he could help in other ways. Adam realised that he no longer wanted to do so purely for self-gain. He actually wanted to help people and make a difference. He could look into creating affordable technology that could be used to help develop cheaper treatments in hospitals for everyday people. Larimore Systems had never taken an interest in science, however, Adam was confident that he could persuade the board to its merits. Eventually the Government would be forced to review their policies as otherwise questions would be asked if they tried to block progress into developing more affordable treatments.

"Mr Larimore?" A woman coming from the opposite direction paused when she recognised him. Her voice drew Adam from his thoughts. "I am so very sorry for your loss. Your father was a well-respected man."

Her choice of words were interesting. Adam had heard 'great' and 'inspirational' a lot and he got the feeling that this woman hadn't been his father's biggest fan. She appeared to be in her late twenties and was wearing a white lab coat and black trousers. She had dark brown almost black hair, and similar colour eyes.

"Thank you," Adam's gaze flitted briefly to the LCD name badge clipped to the front of her lab coat. The screen read 'Dr C Ramirez'.

"Do you need me to call anyone for you?" she ventured apprehensively. This was another misconception as far as normal people were concerned – that Adam Larimore was as unapproachable as his father.

"No thank you. I just needed some time to myself. I'll be heading home in a while."

She seemed relieved and gave him a small smile. "It is quite tranquil watching the water isn't it. That's why I walk to work every day rather than take the tram."

Adam nodded. He'd never really appreciated it before now. "Which hospital do you work at?"

"The South Coast Memorial Hospital in Sector Two," she replied. "I should probably get going. Are you sure you're going to be all right?"

"Yeah," Adam answered softly. It was strange how for the first time he felt as though he had a purpose, a reason for existing other than to be the heir to Larimore Systems. There was much more to Adam than that and a part of him wished that his father was still alive to witness this in the days to come.

CHAPTER ELEVEN

On Saturday morning Raymond Ellison, Victor's solicitor, arrived for the reading of the will.

Ellison was one of six solicitors who worked in the Sector One Central Government Legal Department. All wills were made by appointment and were logged with one of the offices depending on what Sector people lived in. The basic service that left all money, property and possessions to a single relative was charged at a flat fee of six hundred pounds. Any variations were considered extras, as was bequeathing individual items. For those who did not make a will or who could not afford the administration charge, everything was automatically 'inherited' by the Government and supposedly went to the funding of public services. Adam didn't really believe this, not since learning the truth about the L.S.A. He wouldn't be surprised if the money went to financing their underhand activities.

Ellison was a small man in his forties. He spoke in a rather nasal tone that would crack in places the more nervous he became. He'd had several meetings with Adam's father over the years and it had been clear that Victor had intimidated him. He looked uncomfortable now as he opened the file on his computer containing Victor's final will. Wills were sealed in individual files that were locked to thumbprint. These could only be accessed by the solicitor who had assisted in the making of the will it concerned. In addition the file would only become active once a death had been registered. This prevented any unauthorised access or fraud from taking place.

They met in the dining room of Venewood. Adam sat at one end of the real oak dining table. Ellison sat in the middle and Joseph and Eleanor were at the other end. This was merely a formality and Adam almost didn't bother attending at all. The only words he had spoken to his stepbrother since the funeral was that Adam hoped that he'd packed their bags. This had infuriated both Joseph and Eleanor. Legally, however, there was nothing that they could do. Venewood and Larimore Systems now belonged to Adam.

Ivan had been as good as his word and all charges against Adam had been dropped. He had never felt so grateful for this and after returning to Venewood yesterday he had spent the remainder of the day planning his first meeting with the board as the owner of the company. Pitching the new direction would not be easy and Adam did expect some resistance and possible resignations. He didn't care about any of that. In fact Adam would prefer it that way. He was quite capable of running Larimore Systems single-handed and things would move forward a lot faster without having to gain the agreement of greedy and visionless old men.

Ellison apprehensively cleared his throat as he studied the text that the computer screen displayed. Adam leaned back in his chair and shot Joseph a nasty grin. He took back his misgivings about attending this meeting. He was going to enjoy hearing confirmation of his inheritance immensely.

"The last will and testament of Victor James Larimore was recorded ten months ago. Up until then there had been no amendments from the previous version that we held on file. Myself and Ms Sylvia E Underwood, the legal secretary for the department, were witnesses to Mr Larimore's wishes. Now as you can imagine considering the wealth involved this could have potentially taken some time to go through, but in this case there is only one beneficiary."

The idea that the man was stalling suddenly came to Adam and his smirk faded somewhat. Ellison's grey gaze flitted to Adam very quickly and then back down to the computer screen. His shoulders had tensed and he pretended to be reading from the document in front of him again.

"For heaven's sake just read the damn thing!" Eleanor snapped irritably. The grieving widow act had not lasted for long Adam thought to himself. The mention of a sole beneficiary had made them both nervous. Even Adam was surprised. He had thought that his father would make a provision for his wife at least.

"It was Mr Larimore's wish that on the event of his death that his estate in its entirety and ownership of Larimore Systems be left to Joseph Stephen Nichols."

A noise somewhere between a shriek and a gasp escaped Eleanor and a delicate hand flew to her mouth in a bid to disguise this inappropriate response. Adam cast a glance at his stepbrother. Joseph seemed stunned. His jaw had actually dropped and had it been any other situation Adam would have found his reaction incredibly amusing.

"Surely… surely there's some mistake?" Adam found his voice first and hated how shocked and quiet he sounded. There *had* to be a mistake. He had been created to inherit that company! It was his by birth right!

"This is the final will. The estate and business legally belong to Mr Nichols," Ellison replied nervously.

"When the *fuck* did this happen?" Adam demanded as he pushed himself out of his chair with enough force to upend it behind him. He slammed his hands down hard on the table. The computer bounced dangerously and Ellison grabbed it to prevent it from falling.

"I must admit I was rather surprised at his decision, but—"

"No, this isn't right! Your office has made a very serious error, which you will correct immediately."

"There is no error. I am sorry, Mr Larimore. Perhaps if you'd treated your father a bit more kindly he would not have cut you out completely," Ellison said hurriedly as he stood. "Mr Nichols, I will be in touch on Monday to discuss the finer details of the will."

Both Joseph and Eleanor stood, but Ellison shook his head as he shot another wary glance in Adam's direction.

"I can see myself out, thank you."

Adam let him leave. There was no point in arguing with that stuffy official. There had to be a will that superseded it somewhere. There was no way his father would leave *everything* to Joseph. No matter what Adam had done, Larimore Systems was always going to be his company. He'd been created to inherit it. Victor had been under no illusions where Joseph was concerned. Adam's stepbrother knew how to behave and talked a good talk when he wanted to, but he didn't have the intellect, the drive and vision for the business that Adam did. And his father had *known* that. This didn't make any sense.

Before either of them could react Adam ran from the room and up the stairs to his father's office. As Adam raced inside the thought that he hadn't been in here since his father died came to the forefront of his mind. *This was the room where his father had died.* This thought only stopped him for a second. He bit his lip and shook off such sentiments. Adam went to the silver desk and immediately noticed that the inbuilt computer had temporarily been removed. It wasn't Victor's business computer that he was looking for in any case. His father had always had a separate portable one for his personal affairs. Adam opened the lower drawer of the desk and in the bottom he found his own computer. His father must have taken it from his room after throwing him out. Adam left it there and slammed the drawer with enough force to make the entire desk shudder. He opened the second one and then the third. He stood up again and glanced around the neat and orderly room. The only thing on the desk surface was that hideous marble ornament that Adam had given his father for Christmas two years ago. Plutus, the bearded Greek God of Wealth, appeared to frowning and that combined with the somewhat fierce expression in the eyes of the statue had reminded Adam of his father, which was why he'd brought the ornament to begin with. He'd wanted Victor to know how it felt like to have a disapproving glare staring back at him every time he looked at the statue on his desk. Whether he'd made the connection or not Adam never knew. He was tempted to hurl the damn thing at the nearest wall, however, Joseph's sudden appearance in the doorway put paid to that.

"If you're looking for father's computers then you're

wasting your time. Mr Ellison's office have them. As father had a considerable fortune they wanted to ensure that there wasn't a draft will in progress on them prior to the reading. There wasn't by the way."

"This isn't over. I will drag you through the courts if have to. Larimore Systems is my company."

Joseph smirked. "No it isn't. It's mine."

Hearing those words was enough to make him snap. Adam went for Joseph and managed to land a blow to his jaw before the older man could react. Joseph blocked Adam's second attack and used the momentum to shove Adam away. Adam swore and turned his anger on the office itself. There was a digital frame on the wall displaying a photograph of his father, himself, Eleanor and Joseph. Furiously Adam tore it from its hangings and hurled it at the doorway. Joseph had to jump back to avoid being struck. Adam heard a crash in the hallway as it connected with the bannister. The pot plant by the window was his next victim. Adam picked it up and threw it at the right wall. It exploded in a shower of clay and earth.

"Adam!" he heard Eleanor shrieking from somewhere behind him and then, "Oh Joseph do stop him, he's giving me one of my migraines!"

Adam felt an arm encircle his waist and he was dragged forcibly backwards; Joseph's grip on him was too strong for him to fight his way free. Adam cursed and lashed out as his feet left the floor. Joseph grunted in pain although he continued to haul Adam down the stairs and towards the front door. Adam struck the pavement hard as Joseph threw him out onto the street. He glanced up and took some satisfaction upon seeing the blood from his stepbrother's split lip.

"You're no longer welcome here," Joseph told him.

Despite his injury he seemed to take great pleasure in this. Adam climbed to his feet as he struggled to hold back the almost overwhelming fury he felt inside. The extent of his anger actually frightened him. He had to force himself to walk away. Nothing. He had been left with nothing. The final kick in the teeth from his father had been to deny Adam the company that he had been created to inherit. His hatred for the man intensified and that he could do nothing against his father now made it all the more unbearable. He had left Adam without any purpose, any reason for being here. For so long Adam had struggled knowing that he had been engineered for selfish reasons and now he couldn't even have the business that he had been made for.

Adam furiously wiped his eyes as he turned a corner and approached the first public Information Bank and calling system he saw. The Information Bank computer screens were mounted in purpose-built terminals and were activated by a touch screen. The screen then requested that a payment card be pressed inside the rectangle that appeared in the left hand corner of the screen. The Information Bank terminal allowed Internet access, making video calls and withdrawing cash.

The terminal would only allow up to five hundred pounds withdrawal per card and Adam only had one card with him. That would be enough for now. Then Adam made a call.

"Good morning, L.S.A Manchester Office," a young sounding voice answered in a clipped and professional tone. "How may I direct your call?"

"Ivan Williams please."

"I'm afraid Mr Williams is in a meeting. Can I take a message for him?"

Adam had disabled the video feature as he knew that he

looked quite a state. This meant that the receptionist had no idea who she was talking to.

"It's Adam Larimore. I need to speak to him urgently."

There was a long pause and then silence that indicated that Adam had been put on hold. Then he heard his godfather's voice. "Adam, what is it? Are you all right?"

"Did you know?" Adam began without giving Ivan much time to say anything else.

"Know what?"

"That father left the entire estate to Joseph?"

There was a sharp intake of breath and then silence from the older man.

"Ivan!" Adam demanded impatiently.

"No, of course not. I don't understand why he'd do such a thing," Ivan insisted hurriedly.

"Because he hated me," Adam snapped. "He's left me with nothing, Ivan. And Joseph's kicked me out."

Again there was a lengthy pause. "Margaret and I will be back in two days. Do you have somewhere you can stay until then?"

"I think so. Ivan—"

"I have to go, Adam, I'm in rather an important meeting. Please wait until I get back and then we can sort this out together. Joseph isn't an unreasonable man and he knows what an asset you are to Larimore Systems. I'm sure you'll still have a job there if you want it."

Adam almost laughed at this. There was no way that Joseph would ever let him near Larimore Systems again.

"I know it seems as though the world has ended, Adam, but it hasn't," Ivan continued in an attempt to calm him when he realised that his assurances about a job prospect hadn't had the reaction that he had been hoping for. "You're a very bright and talented young man with so many options. Your father knew this too. Perhaps he was trying to give you a choice in life? A chance to take a different path."

Adam silently shook his head. He very much doubted that. "Thanks, Ivan. I'll give you a call in a couple of days."

"Good. Now please don't do anything until I get back," Ivan reiterated firmly.

"I won't," Adam sighed. He knew that Ivan was worried he might do something stupid. Adam hadn't actually ruled out going back to Venewood and confronting Joseph again. That bastard had thrown him out with nothing aside from the clothes he was wearing!

"Look after yourself, Adam."

"Thanks, Ivan," he murmured softly as he ended the call. Whilst he appreciated Ivan's kindness it hadn't helped with his upset. Adam sighed and stepped away from the Information Bank. With Ivan away at the moment there was only one other place he could think of going so Adam caught the next tram to old Tower Hamlets. He was so preoccupied with his thoughts that he barely registered the walk once he disembarked; only his arrival at his destination. Thankfully he had been given the code to the apartment block and so Adam didn't need to call up to be let in. There was a man in the foyer who gave him a curious glance, but he did not say anything. Before his father had died Adam would have been worried about being seen here. Now this no longer mattered.

Adam reached the top of the stairs and knocked on his lover's apartment door.

"Adam?" Leon exclaimed, not bothering to conceal his surprise. The blond had clearly still been in bed despite it being near to lunchtime. He wasn't wearing a shirt and his trousers had clearly been pulled on in a hurry as he was still buttoning them as he opened the door.

"Can I come in?" Adam requested softly. They hadn't spoken since Adam's father had died.

"Yeah sure," Leon stepped aside to permit Adam entrance. He led him back through to his bedroom.

"I'm sorry to hear about your old man," the blond said uncomfortably as he sat down on the bed. "How are you holding up?"

"Okay I guess," Adam sat down beside his lover. "I'm sorry I didn't call you. I wanted too, but I couldn't…things have been difficult."

"You don't have to apologise," Leon reached out and brushed some of the hair from Adam's face in a seemingly tender act. "I figured you'd need your space."

Adam sighed and leaned into the contact. "Thanks. Do you have work later?"

"No I'm not on the rota for today," Leon shook his head.

"Would you mind if I stayed here for a couple of days?" Adam was reluctant to tell Leon about the will. He wasn't sure how his lover would react and in any case hopefully Ivan would sort it out without the need for many people to know.

"Sure," Leon agreed. He seemed somewhat hesitant although he did lean over to kiss Adam after replying. Adam automatically returned his kiss and wrapped his arms around Leon, although if he was honest his heart wasn't in it or where Leon wanted it to lead. When Adam felt Leon lowering him back onto the bed he pulled away.

"Sorry," he murmured. "I can't…"

"It's okay," Leon said softly as he sat up. "You're all over the place, that's understandable. Why don't you get some sleep?"

"Wait," Adam caught hold of his arm. "Can you stay?"

This request clearly took Leon by surprise although he did lie back down on the bed. Adam moved closer to Leon until he was resting his head against Leon's shoulder. He felt Leon wrap his arms around him. Lying here like this almost made him forget about all that had happened. Almost.

"I love you." Those three little words escaped him before Adam actually realised what he was saying. And he meant them. Leon clearly realised he did too.

"Adam, we've been through this," Leon said with a sigh as he pulled away and sat up. "I don't want a relationship, and I didn't think you did either."

Adam bit his lip as he glanced at his lover. "I didn't think I could have one before. Now that's changed. Don't you even want to consider it?"

"I'm leaving," Leon answered shortly. "At the end of the week actually."

"Leaving?" Adam demanded. "Where are you going?"

"I've got a transfer to a warehouse in Birmingham. There's more hours and housing for workers is provided."

"Were you going to tell me?" Adam asked whilst trying to conceal just how much this actually upset him.

Leon shrugged as he got up from the bed. He seemed somewhat uncomfortable at least. "I didn't think it would bother you. It's not like you're gonna find it difficult to meet someone else."

"I could come with you?" Adam suggested. This surprised him as much as it did Leon. After everything he had already lost, Adam couldn't bear to lose Leon too.

“You’ve got a company to run,” Leon said finally.

“What if I didn’t?” Adam pressed as he moved so that he was sitting on the end of the bed.

“Adam—”

“I didn’t inherit Larimore Systems,” he blurted this out more in desperation than anything to counter the excuses that Leon made. Adam swallowed hard as he tentatively awaited the blond’s reaction.

“What are you talking about?” Leon asked carefully. His neutral tone and expression made it difficult for Adam to gauge his feelings on the matter.

“Joseph inherited the company and my father’s money. He left me with nothing.”

“I’m sorry,” Leon replied finally. “This doesn’t change how I feel.”

“And how do you feel?” Adam asked. He wasn’t certain that he wanted to hear Leon’s answer.

“I don’t want a relationship with you.”

“Why not?” Adam asked softly.

“Don’t get me wrong, you’re fucking hot and everything, but…do I have to really say this?”

“Yeah,” Adam answered in annoyance. “You do.”

“You kind of act like a spoilt brat most of the time. You’re completely self-obsessed and let’s face it, even though you say you hate the idea that you were genetically engineered for a single purpose, you think you’re so much better than everyone else. I don’t think you care about me. I don’t think you care about anyone other than yourself.”

“I didn’t realise you felt that way about me,” Adam replied quietly.

The blond sighed. “We had fun together; I’m not

denying that. I just don't like you enough as a person to want to be with you."

His words had cut deep. Adam had hoped that Leon had felt something for him. Even if it wasn't love; to know that Leon cared about him would have been enough. To hear that the blond felt nothing at all, that Adam had just been entertainment to him was horrible. He had been used. Leon, like everyone else, had taken advantage of him and then cast him aside without a second thought.

I love you

Adam winced as he suddenly felt terribly foolish and naïve. It should have been obvious that Leon cared little for him. He hadn't even come to the hospital when Adam had been shot whilst making sure that Leon had got away. The blond hadn't even really mentioned it. Leon had just shrugged it off like it was nothing. Like Adam was nothing.

He drew a breath as he struggled to contain his emotions. As much as Adam wanted to make Leon feel as bad as he did, a part of him didn't want his lover to see just how upset he was.

"Okay," he said quietly as he stood. "Good luck with your new life."

"Adam," Leon caught his arm as he hurried to the door. "Don't run out like this. I'm just trying to be honest with you." Leon gave him an uncertain smile, "We had fun, didn't we?"

Adam roughly pulled away. "Fuck you, Leon," he snarled before leaving the apartment. What the hell did he expect after saying something like that? Leon didn't follow him downstairs and Adam was torn between feeling relief at this and disappointment that the blond had let him go.

CHAPTER TWELVE

"I thought you said you had somewhere to stay?"

The dismay on his godfather's face caused Adam to wince. He managed a small shake of his head and murmured, "It didn't work out," as he stepped inside. Since leaving Leon's apartment Adam had been sleeping rough in what remained of Hyde Park. Much of the park had been destroyed and redevelopment had been a slow process due to lack of funding. Currently only a small sector near to the Serpentines riverbed had been replanted.

There were few visitors to the park and thankfully Adam been able to keep a low profile. His upset over Leon was mainly clouded with anger at his cruel words. Deep down Adam had suspected that he was being used and despite being proved right it had still hurt. He considered finding out exactly where Leon's new job was and using any remaining influence he had to screw things up for him. Then he'd know how it felt to have absolutely nothing. Yet even the thought of this didn't bring Adam the satisfaction that he thought it would. Because even after everything a part of Adam still loved Leon.

"I had the clothes you left here laundered for you. They're in the spare bedroom," Ivan's voice drew Adam from his thoughts. "Why don't you have a shower and get changed. I'll get you something to eat and then we can have a chat."

"Have you sorted it out?" Adam asked, hope sparking inside of him.

"Get yourself cleaned up and then we can talk," Ivan responded. He gave Adam a forced smile and gently squeezed his shoulder. Adam sighed knowing that this was all he would get from him until Ivan was ready.

He went through to the spare room and found a pair of his black jeans, a black shirt and underwear. Adam took these through to the bathroom. Despite his want to address the matter of the will immediately Adam had to admit he was starting to feel better as he stepped under the warm spray of the shower. He was mildly disgusted at the amount of dirt that intermingled with the water and pooled at his feet before commencing the sluggish spiral down the drain. Adam borrowed a pine scented shower gel from the shelf on the side of the shower wall. He couldn't find any shampoo within easy reach so he washed his hair with the gel too. He was feeling more like his old self again when he finally got out of the shower. Adam dried himself off and put on his change of clothes. He only towel dried his hair briefly before eagerly making his way back into the living room. Ivan had heated up a tomato pasta bake for him. Adam hadn't realised how hungry he was until then. He sat on the sofa in silence whilst quickly devouring the meal. Then he became aware of Ivan sitting down beside him. His godfather took the empty plate and cutlery from him and set them down on the table.

"Where's Margaret?" Adam asked, suddenly noting her absence for the first time.

"She's at the hospital having a scan. I really ought to be with her but…" for a brief second Adam saw a glimmer of a different man; a man barely holding onto his emotions. Then it was gone. Ivan cleared his throat, most likely to dislodge the lump forming in it.

"Is she going to be all right?" Adam tentatively asked.

"They've caught it early, which I'm told is a good thing."

Even though his godfather hadn't clarified exactly what was wrong, from judging from Ivan's reaction Adam could hazard a good guess.

"I've spoken to Raymond Ellison," Ivan said, changing the subject. "Unfortunately the will is legal and appears to be the last one that Victor made."

"But I can challenge it?" Adam asked.

Ivan sighed. "You could in theory, after all you are Victor's only blood relative. I asked Mr Ellison if a challenge would be successful. In your case he doubts that it would be. There is no evidence to suggest that Victor was coerced into making that will or that he was suffering from an illness that might explain a lapse in judgement. In fact it was pointed out to me by several individuals that Victor may have made that will because thanks to your behaviour he believed that his company was safer in Joseph's hands."

This was not what Adam wanted to hear at all. "So basically there's nothing you can do," he snapped angrily.

"I've spent hours trying, Adam. I've come up against a wall at the end of every avenue I've gone down. In the end I decided to speak to Joseph directly."

Adam snorted and leaned back on the sofa. "I bet that was

a waste of time."

"At the board meeting yesterday Joseph terminated your employment with Larimore Systems in your absence, as I expected he would."

"That bastard! I'll—"

"Adam!" Ivan interrupted in annoyance. He held up his hand to silence his godson and waited several seconds before continuing. "I pointed out that surely Victor never intended for you to have nothing to do with the company and that you are the reason that it has gone from strength to strength in recent years. Ultimately Joseph refused to heed my advice. He did, however, agree that you could return to Venewood this afternoon to collect your belongings."

"Well that's big of him," Adam sneered.

"All this nastiness could have been avoided if you'd just made an effort to tolerate him," Ivan pointed out tiredly. "Now I've pulled some strings and I've managed to get you an apartment in the Chrysalis development in Sector One."

"The Chrysalis development?" Adam repeated hesitantly. That was the new development that was strictly for Government officials and L.S.A staff. From what he'd heard it was a luxury apartment block with a hot tub room in each room, a gymnasium in the basement and services that included cooking and laundry. "How did you get me a place there?"

"I'm the Chief of Police," Ivan reminded him. "That means that I am entitled to certain privileges."

"Still it's a pretty big favour."

"It is," Ivan nodded. "Adam, remember what you said to me the day of Victor's funeral? Don't let what's happened with the will change that. You'll go far in life with or without the Larimore fortune."

"You still want me to join the L.S.A when you're promoted?"

"If I'm promoted," Ivan corrected unhappily. "Jeff Ingham still has reservations."

Adam knew this was, in part, down to him and he felt bad for this. His godfather had wanted this for as long as Adam could remember. He also thought about his recent discoveries concerning the L.S.A. He wondered what Ivan's reaction would be if he knew the truth. Still he said nothing. Now was not the right time to bring it up.

"You're the only choice, Ivan," he assured his godfather.

"I hope so. Will you reconsider my offer, Adam?"

"No," Adam shook his head. No matter how bad things got he was not going to join the L.S.A knowing what he did about them. Ivan looked disappointed and frustrated so Adam quickly changed the subject. "Are you coming to Venewood with me?"

"No. I need to be with Margaret. Joseph said that you can come after lunch. Anything you can't carry he's agreed to arrange to be forwarded. Despite what he says now I'm certain that in a few months he will realise his mistake, if the board don't point it out first."

"The board aren't exactly fans of mine either."

"No, but they're not stupid. They know how important you are to the company's future."

Adam didn't hold out much hope of support from the board. When his father was alive they were purely a formality and a source of irritation for him. The board would certainly have more of a say in the company's future now than they would have had with Adam as the owner. A part of him still couldn't quite believe that this was happening. That company had defined him since he was born. If he couldn't fight for it then he was going to make sure that Joseph paid dearly for his stolen inheritance.

***

The reception that Adam received upon his return to Venewood was cold. Eleanor answered the door and only permitted him to stand in the hallway whilst she went to get Joseph. The pretence of the grieving widow was gone now that her future was secure. She looked at Adam was though he was nothing. This was further proof that she'd never loved Adam's father at all. If she had then she wouldn't have seen his son out on the streets and cut off from everything that he had been created to inherit.

Joseph was equally as nasty. He looked at Adam with disgust and the loathing was more than mutual.

"You have ten minutes," Joseph told him.

"Whatever," Adam glowered angrily at him before ascending the stairs. Already Venewood felt as though it were a strange place. It had never really felt like home to begin with and even less so now. It was cold and unwelcoming. If Adam had inherited it then he would have had it pulled down. A luxury apartment was much more him than an old-fashioned mansion that offered him nothing besides pain and regret. Losing the company hurt more and despite what Ivan had said, Adam couldn't let that go. He would find a way to get it back.

He went into his room and saw that everything was more or less where he had left it. The only thing that had changed was that the bed had been stripped of its sheets.

Adam had brought with him a large grey bag, which

wasn't nearly big enough for all his clothes let alone anything else. He had a quick browse through his wardrobe and selected his favourite outfits. Being aware of the time limit and that Joseph would certainly make sure that he kept to it, Adam hurriedly shoved the clothes into his bag before going over to his desk. He put his media capsules into the bag and then looked around for his computer. He frowned when he couldn't see it anywhere. Then he recalled that it was in his father's office. Adam left his bag in his bedroom doorway and hurried back along the hall. He hoped that he could slip inside without Joseph noticing. Unfortunately he was not going to be that lucky.

"Where are you going?" Joseph demanded from the bottom of the stairs.

"I left some things in father's office," Adam replied without stopping. To his annoyance his stepbrother came up the stairs and followed him into the other room.

"Raymond returned the computers yesterday. There is no alternative will." Joseph had misinterpreted his actions and he clearly had no idea that Ivan had already checked for this. "Father's last will is final. He wanted me to run Larimore Systems."

Despite himself Adam couldn't help snapping back at him. "The board will never—"

"The board doesn't have a choice. The documentation is legal. They can either work with me or walk. Either way I don't care. As I said at the meeting your employment and directorship is terminated with immediate effect. Just be grateful I'm letting you come back to *my* home to collect your things."

That smug bastard thought that he'd won. Well he'd soon

realise just how wrong he was.

Adam whirled around and roughly shoved the older man backwards. "Don't worry I'll be out of your way soon enough."

Adam then turned his attention back to retrieving his computer. He walked quickly over to his father's desk and as he had hoped it was still in the drawer. He shot Joseph an angry look as he walked by, but his stepbrother abruptly reached out and pulled the computer from his hands.

"I'm afraid that's property of Larimore Systems. It contains valuable information does it not? As you are an ex-employee I can't let you take that."

"You know full well it has nothing of intellectual value on there," Adam retaliated. He took a step forward and attempted to snatch it back from the taller man. Joseph easily evaded him and shoved Adam away. Adam stumbled and as he did so he saw red. Was it not enough for Joseph that Adam had been cut out of the estate? He wanted to take everything that Adam had! On that computer was all the secrets of the L.S.A and programs that Adam was developing including his Aether computer system. He was *not* going to leave Venewood without it.

"Maybe not, but it was still purchased for business use so you can't keep it," Joseph sneered at him as he avoided another attempt that Adam made to grab it back.

"Fuck you." Adam then spat on him. From experience he knew it would only antagonise his stepbrother, however, the overwhelming anger and frustration he was feeling wouldn't let him consider any repercussions. Joseph struck him and even though Adam had expected this it still hurt. He fell back a few paces as his hand reached up to touch his split lower lip.

The cut would heal within a few moments and this would further enrage Joseph. He hated that any wounds he inflicted when they fought would soon disappear whilst any blows that Adam dealt him would take days, if not a week, to fade.

"No wonder father left me in charge," he seethed as he continued to move towards Adam. "Look at you. What a disappointment you were for him."

"Better a disappointment than his mindless clone," Adam retorted as he backed up further to keep some space between them. "All you ever did was nod in favour of his every word. Father only left you in charge to spite me. He never intended for you to continue without me. He knew as well as you do that I *am* Larimore Systems. All the technological advances and money made in recent years are down to me."

"You're absolutely full of it. Do you think for a moment that I am incapable of managing—"

"Yes! I'll go off and make millions on my own as your competitor. Within six months you'll be begging me to come back."

This remark was designed to infuriate Joseph more, mainly because it was true. Adam was perfectly capable of setting up a rival company and burying Larimore Systems, and Joseph knew this even if he wouldn't admit it.

"You seem very sure of yourself, but do you know how father really saw you? As a freak. His failure of a science project. He'd often talk to me about what a disappointment you were. It was practically his last act to throw you out of his home! He hated you!"

You don't act it. You are a constant disappointment to me, a failure. I had hoped that thanks to science I could have the heir that I always wanted. A perfect son to pass on the mantle and continue the Larimore family business. But instead I ended up with you.

Adam lashed out as these cruel words echoing his father's brought back all the pain and unresolved feelings in a rush. He smashed his fist into Joseph's jaw with as much weight behind the blow as he could muster. He thought he heard something crack as his stepbrother retaliated. He caught Adam round the face with a counter punch that left his ears ringing. The computer fell onto the floor as he fought back. Joseph managed to block this punch and the next. Adam gasped when Joseph's fist made painful contact with his stomach. He almost doubled over and wasn't able to avoid the strike that caught him on the left side of his head. Adam gasped as his vision momentarily went dark. He was aware that he'd fallen against his father's desk. He heard Joseph behind him and suddenly his stepbrother had seized hold of his wrists. He forced Adam's arms out in front of him and used his bodyweight to pin Adam against the furniture. His cheek scraped the cold surface as Adam tried in vain to free himself. Joseph's grip on his wrists was almost crushing and in that moment Adam actually felt afraid. This had already gone too far. Usually his father would interrupt them before a fight got too serious, and Adam doubted that Eleanor would help him. She wouldn't care if Joseph killed him. Adam again tried to free himself. He twisted his arms in an attempt to force Joseph to let him go. The older man swore under his breath as his grip tightened.

"Do you know what else father told me about you?" he breathed close to Adam's ear. His voice had taken on a darker edge to it, one that left Adam feeling cold. "That you like to be fucked by other men. Let's see if that's true shall we?"

"Get off of me!" Adam's anger gave way to blind panic as he felt Joseph's free hand slide round to attempt to undo the zip on his jeans. Adam began to thrash about on the desk trying in absolute desperation to free himself. But the vicelike grip on his wrists remained, although his struggles meant that Joseph couldn't do much else other than hold him still. Adam's heart was beating so hard in his chest that it hurt. The panic taking over him made him blind to his surroundings. All he could feel was the weight on him and the desk beneath him, and no matter how hard he fought he could not force Joseph off of him. His stepbrother had the advantage in both the situation and physically also.

Finally Joseph became tired of his struggling and struck him. Adam immediately went limp against the desk. Feigning submission was the only chance he had to stop this. He forced his body to relax and even whimpered slightly much to Joseph's delight. As he predicted Adam felt the grip on his wrists relax and then release completely. He struggled hard not to tense when he felt hands undoing his jeans. Adam's gaze flitted to the object on the desk just within his grasp. The statue of Plutus was glaring severely back at him and for a moment he imagined it was the face of his father.

You deserve this...all of this...

No, Adam thought to himself, I don't! As Joseph pulled Adam's jeans and underwear down he struck. He moved too quickly for the older man to react. Adam felt the cold marble against his palm as he grabbed hold of the statue. He whirled around, swinging it in a downward arch as he did so. There was a dull thud as Plutus caught Joseph on the right side of his head. Immediately he collapsed, falling back onto the floor with another thud. Adam dropped the statue onto the carpet as he stumbled away from his father's desk. The tears that filled his eyes were a combination of shock and relief. Only then did he realise that he was shaking. He pulled his clothes back up and it was several attempts with shaking fingers before he could successfully fasten his jeans. What Joseph had tried to do…even Adam hadn't thought him capable of that. He sniffed and wiped his eyes as he turned his attention to his almost rapist. Joseph was lying on his back exactly where he had fallen. Adam took a cautious step closer; he was afraid that Joseph would jump up and attack him again. Then he saw the blood.

"Joseph?" Adam called quietly. Joseph's head was tilted slightly to the side and Adam could see the wound that he'd inflicted. The hair around the injury was matted with blood and Adam gagged when he saw pieces of white amongst the crimson. The blow had caved the skull inwards and there was too much blood and fragments of bone for Adam to see it clearly. Feeling sick he cast his gaze up to Joseph's face. His grey eyes were fixated on the ceiling above and no light was reflecting in them. He was dead. The blow had killed him.

Adam's hand flew to his mouth in utter horror as he stumbled backwards away from the body. He'd just wanted to stun him, to make Joseph let him go. He hadn't meant to kill him…or had he? Adam had been angry enough. Joseph had taken everything from him. Perhaps he had wanted to… No! Adam wasn't a murderer. He could never have imagined himself taking a life.

But you have…you've smashed his skull in…he was alive not seconds before and now he's dead. Because of you.

It was self-defence, Adam chanted inside his head over and over again as he backed away from Joseph's body. It was an accident. A terrible, horrible accident.

"Joe?" Adam's pounding heart almost stopped when he heard Eleanor's voice and then her rapid approach. He knew he ought to stop her, but he couldn't. He couldn't do anything other than watch helplessly as the scene unfolded around him.

"Are you all right? I heard shouting? Has Adam gone yet? The sooner he leaves the better. I know the doctors said that Victor's heart attack was not stress related but that selfish boy couldn't have helped. It wouldn't surprise me if—" Her complaining abruptly cut off into an anguished scream. Adam flinched, barely able to watch as Eleanor raced to her son's side.

"Joe? Oh god, Joseph!"

Adam fell back against the desk that he'd previously been so desperate to move away from. He felt sick as he watched Eleanor cradling Joseph to her. The front of her white dress quickly became smeared with his blood and this combined with her sobs and screams was unbearable. Adam sniffed as he fought to hold back his tears and this noise drew his stepmother's attention.

"What did you do?" she demanded with wide and pain-filled eyes as her grip on Joseph tightened.

"He attacked me…" Adam struggled to speak, his voice barely above a whisper as he fought against the lump that had formed in his throat. "I didn't mean to…"

"You killed him."

"I didn't mean—"

"You killed him!" Eleanor shrieked as she scrambled to her feet. Joseph's body fell back onto the carpet. His head was now turned to the side and Adam had to look away from the lifeless grey eyes staring accusingly at him.

You killed him...

Hearing that was unbearable. Adam hadn't meant to do it. As much as he hated Joseph he had not wanted to kill him. Why couldn't she see that? Did she really think he was that much of a monster?

"Please," Adam begged, his voice wavering dangerously. "I didn't mean to do it. He..." Adam trailed off as his stepmother turned to flee the room.

Eleanor wouldn't even give him a chance to explain! She had to hear him out Adam thought in panic as he gave chase. He grabbed hold of his stepmother as she reached the door. Her reaction to his touch was nothing short of utter terror.

"Get off of me! Murderer!"

"Please let me explain!" Adam pleaded as his grip tightened. She *had* to let him explain. This wasn't his fault...he hadn't meant to... Adam winced, recoiling as she slapped him. This stunned him only enough to allow her a small head start.

"Wait!" Adam implored as he raced after her. Eleanor had reached the top step of the stairs when Adam caught her. He grabbed her wrist and jerked her around.

"Let me go!" Eleanor cried out in fright. She raised a hand and caught Adam across the cheek. Her painted nails cut across his skin and the shock of the sudden pain caused him to roughly shove her backwards. The next couple of seconds seemed to Adam as though they were occurring in slow motion. Eleanor's tearstained face twisted in an expression of shock and then utter terror as she lost her footing. She tumbled backwards down the stairs. Every thud of her delicate frame against the wood caused Adam to flinch. A black high-heeled shoe fell from her left foot and tumbled down before her.

Down she went until her head struck the marble tile at the bottom of the staircase with a horrible crack. Adam stared on in silence, feeling barely able to breathe. He willed for her to move, to show some sign of life. But as with her son the ever expanding pool of crimson beneath her head confirmed what deep down Adam already knew. Eleanor Larimore was dead.

At this realisation Adam felt his legs go out from underneath him. He sobbed, desperately clutching at the stair rail as he slid down to lean against it. He'd killed them both.

"I'm sorry, I'm so sorry," Adam whimpered. It was a terrible accident. He hadn't wanted to kill either of them. This went round and round in his head until Adam felt he couldn't take it anymore. He sobbed harder and gripped the rails so tightly that it hurt until eventually he lost track of time. He remained in his position at the top of the stairs racked with guilt and grief. He didn't mean for this to happen. Adam would never have wished them dead let alone contemplated killing them.

Then finally one rational thought surfaced amongst all the panic and horror. He had to call for help. This Adam resisted until the quiet voice became an insistence that refused to be ignored. Who could he call? Who would believe him? Even with the security footage showing Joseph attempting to rape him it could be argued that Adam used unnecessary force to disable his attacker because of his father's will. And that he then feigned panic in order to murder Eleanor. No one would believe that it was purely self-defence and an accident. Adam had been violent in the past. He would be convicted and imprisoned for life. Adam couldn't take that. He knew he couldn't cope with prison. Memories of those horrid days in the cell before his father's funeral came to the forefront of his mind. He couldn't do it again. And why should he? He was as much as victim as they were.

But you killed them...they didn't deserve to die...

No, Adam told himself, they hadn't, but it had been an accident. A tragic accident.

Adam drew a shaky breath and forced himself to stand. There was only one person he could trust. Reluctantly he returned to his father's office. He remained focused on the desk and not Joseph's body otherwise he'd lose the little composure that he had regained. Adam swallowed hard and touched the computer screen in order to activate it. The security program was locked by thumbprint recognition and could only be accessed by a member of the household. Thankfully Adam still had clearance. A standard protocol to prevent anyone manipulating the footage was to automatically delete it if an attempt to copy it was made. However, Adam knew how to get around this. He could trick the system into thinking it was being installed onto a new computer. It would mean that it was wiped from the computer here. That didn't matter. Adam only needed to show it to Ivan. Ivan would believe him without question. Only Ivan could be trusted.

Adam retrieved his computer and transferred all the footage from this afternoon. A message on screen confirmed that it was deleted from the main system. As his computer did not have the auto delete feature he was also able to make a copy on a media capsule as a backup. It had just completed when he heard a knock at the front door. Adam hurriedly checked the real-time security feed and he felt panic welling up inside of him when he saw a policeman standing the other side of it. Adam froze, feeling as though he was going to breakdown at any moment. What was he going to do?

Venewood only had the front exit. If he tried to run then he'd be shot or arrested, perhaps both. Adam forced himself to take a couple of deep breaths. He had some time. There was no way the policeman knew what had happened here. This worked to Adam's advantage. He slipped the media capsule into his pocket and retrieved his computer. He left the office and closed the door behind him. Adam quickly hurried down the hallway to his bedroom to retrieve his bag. He put his computer inside before heading downstairs.

He refused to look at Eleanor as he carefully stepped over her body. He couldn't avoid treading in her blood and Adam flinched at the dark red footprints that followed him. He set his bag down in the corner out of sight before answering the door.

"Sorry to disturb you, Mr Larimore, we received a call from a member of the public who thought they heard a disturbance. Is everything okay here?"

The policeman was in his early twenties and Adam suspected he was quite new to his job. Still this didn't mean that Adam would be able to keep up his pretence for long.

Adam quickly shook his head. His anxiety and barely holding back of tears were not faked. He stepped aside to reveal Eleanor's still form. "She fell. I tried to help her..."

The police officer – Officer Chandra – immediately entered and went to Eleanor.

"Mrs Larimore?" he called as he pressed two fingers against her neck. Adam started to move quietly towards him. He willed Officer Chandra to remain crouched over Eleanor, but at the last minute Adam's approach was heard.

Officer Chandra drew his gun although he didn't manage to raise the weapon before Adam hit him. He fell down beside

Eleanor's body and his weapon slid from his hand. Adam grabbed it and quickly raised it level with Officer Chandra's head. The man's youth and lack of experience showed as he pleaded, "Don't shoot. Please..."

Adam silently shook his head. Officer Chandra thought that he was a killer without even questioning him. It was what all of them would think. He wouldn't even be given a chance. He began to back away, keeping the gun raised as he reached the door. Adam carefully knelt down to grab his bag. Once he had it he backed out of the door and pressed the tile on the wall outside to close it. Then he turned and fled knowing that he probably had barely minutes to get clear of this street before police backup arrived.

Adam took off down the main street. He continued running until he turned a corner onto the next block. Only then did he slow to a brisk walk. Thankfully the bloody footprints he had initially left in his wake had faded. All appeared to be normal although a couple of passers-by gave him some curious stares. He wasn't approached and Adam felt some anxiety subsiding. He just had to keep moving and not think too much about the scene that he had left behind. The first thing he had to do was find somewhere to lie low. As soon as the news broke Adam would be hunted by every single policeman and L.S.A agent in the capital. He needed to find somewhere quickly.

Even though much of Sector One was populated Adam knew of a few sites where regeneration had been halted due to finance being an issue. These were on the outskirts and the city's homeless often used them as shelters. These could have been a possibility, but Adam was concerned that he might be recognised and turned in by one of them for the reward money that would undoubtedly be offered. There was, however, another option.

There were plenty of newly built and unoccupied properties in this sector. The security on them was supposedly infallible, but not for Adam's Aether program. He knew roughly where several of these new blocks of flats were and he turned into the direction of one now. As Adam walked he struggled to maintain his composure and fight away thoughts of what had occurred. Ivan would help him, he told himself over and over. He just had to hold it together until he was able to get to Ivan's apartment. That was all he had to do.

CHAPTER THIRTEEN

Adam bit his lip as he cast a wary glance around him and then back to the rapidly scrolling computer screen.

"Come on," he whispered urgently as the program continued to communicate with the security system on the apartment door. As Adam had suspected there had been a full-scale manhunt for him and he had been forced to lay low in one of the newly completed apartment blocks in Sector Two. However, after two days in hiding he'd become increasingly desperate and, fearful of discovery, Adam had decided to chance it. By some miracle and with the cover of darkness Adam managed to make it to Ivan's home unseen. Yet much to Adam's dismay when he arrived Ivan wasn't there so Adam had decided to break in. Thankfully he'd thought to take his computer with him and the Aether system appeared to have no trouble in accessing the security system for the apartment. The time seemed to crawl by and every second made Adam more and more agitated. Finally there was a bleep and the front door slid open. Hurriedly Adam went inside and shut the door behind him.

The apartment was dark and at first Adam was hesitant about switching the lights on. But he couldn't just stand there in the darkness. He didn't want to alarm Ivan when he returned. Adam swallowed hard as he pressed the tile on the wall to activate the lights in the living room. The apartment had always felt almost clinical to Adam and even more so now. He moved slowly over to the sofa and sat down on it. Disappointment that Ivan wasn't here filled him as he buried his face in his hands. For the last two days all he had thought about was that afternoon at Venewood. It was all he could see whenever he closed his eyes.

"Get off of me! Murderer!"

"Please let me explain!" Adam pleaded as his grip tightened. She had to let him explain. This wasn't his fault...he hadn't meant to... Adam winced, recoiling as she slapped him. This stunned him only enough to allow her a small head start.

"Wait!" Adam implored as he raced after her. Eleanor had reached the top step of the stairs when Adam caught her. He grabbed her wrist and jerked her around.

"Let me go!" Eleanor cried out in fright. She raised a hand and caught Adam across the cheek. Her painted nails cut across his skin and the shock of the sudden pain caused him to roughly shove her backwards. The next couple of seconds seemed to Adam as though they were occurring in slow motion. Eleanor's tearstained face twisted in an expression of shock and then utter terror as she lost her footing.

Adam gasped out loud, flinching as the image of Eleanor's panicked and terrified face remained long after he had opened his eyes. He would always see that face. Adam knew this. He would never be able to shake it no matter how much he tried.

The memories of her expression moments before she fell would be crystal clear in his mind forever and a part of Adam felt as though he deserved that. Even though Eleanor had treated him horribly he had never wanted to hurt her.

Joseph's death he had begun to rationalise and come to terms with what he'd done. If he hadn't then Joseph would have raped him and could have possibly killed him. Even though Adam hadn't meant to deliver a fatal blow he couldn't feel quite as terrible about it as he did Eleanor's death.

After some time Adam found himself growing restless. He had assumed that Margaret was still at the hospital, and Adam was reluctant to call Ivan in case he alerted anyone else to his whereabouts. Adam got up from the sofa and made his way over to a door on the left leading off from the living quarters. This was Ivan's office; a room that Adam had never been permitted to enter. Thinking that he might be able to access the computer and get some information about the police hunt for him Adam pressed the tile on the wall to open the door. Immediately it asked for a numerical password. Adam didn't bother with trying to guess it. He connected his computer to the port to the right of the tile. Aether's decrypting software opened the door in seconds. As it slid open Adam stepped inside. The light sensor reacted to his presence and it came on automatically. The office was small and housed only a metal silver-finished desk with an inbuilt computer running the Eos system and a houseplant in a tub next to the door. There were a couple of digital photo frames on the wall to the right of the desk. The top photo was taken on Ivan and Margaret's wedding day. Adam's father, as the best man, stood to Ivan's left. There was also a photo of Ivan with his father and another of Ivan receiving his promotion as Chief of Police.

However, it was the final photo that caught Adam's eye. It was of Ivan, Margaret and a young man close to Adam's age, most likely only a few years older. He had ash-blond hair that just brushed the nape of his neck. His eyes were a cool light blue, almost grey, and seemed to flash in merriment at the camera. He had one arm around Margaret. His other arm was at his side. Ivan had his hand on the man's shoulder. Margaret was looking at the young man rather than the camera. Her expression resembled that of a proud parent; this wasn't possible. Ivan and Margaret didn't have a son. Then who was this? Ivan had never mentioned anyone matching the young man's description. Adam shook his head slightly as he forced himself to dismiss it. How was this even relevant? He was wasting valuable time.

Adam was beside the desk when he heard a door opening. He felt relief as he recognised Ivan's step. In a few minutes this nightmare would be half over.

The office door had remained open and Ivan paused as he came to the threshold. His expression seemed tense and somewhat confused. He wasn't that pleased to see Adam standing there. Adam tensed as he waited for his godfather to speak.

"Half of the police force and the L.S.A are looking for you. How did you get in here?" Ivan's tone was clipped and one that he usually reserved for lower ranking officials and police officers; not for someone he'd known since birth or that he ought to care about.

Adam forced a small smile despite the cool reception. "I disabled your security system," he admitted softly.

"What do you want?" Ivan asked as he entered the room. He closed the door behind him and even now his cold expression refused to soften. Adam felt the tears that he'd tried to hold back until now start to fall. He didn't understand this at all. Why was Ivan treating him as though he were a stranger, or worse a criminal?

"I…I need your help," he managed to choke out. This brought about an irritated sigh from the older man.

"I've been helping you, Adam. Every time you've gotten into trouble I've been able to protect you until now."

"I know," Adam answered shakily. He kept his gaze on his godfather as Ivan drew closer to him. Ivan didn't know the truth yet, that was why he was being so cold Adam tried to tell himself over and over.

"Do you also realise that my obligation to you ended when your father, my closest friend, died?" Ivan questioned in obvious displeasure.

Obligation? Was that all Adam was to him? An unwanted responsibility? He thought back to his father's funeral and how Ivan had comforted him afterwards. Ivan was like a father to him and Adam had thought that Ivan saw him more as a son than an 'obligation'.

"I do," he managed to force out finally. "But this is a terrible mistake. I've got the security footage to prove it."

Ivan's detachment wavered at this information. "Why didn't you bring this to light sooner?"

"Because most of the officers on the force want to lock me up and throw away the key. I don't trust any of them, but I trust you. You're my godfather, Ivan," Adam knew he was all but pleading now. Fear and upset were the dominating emotions inside of him and he didn't know which one to give into. This wasn't how he'd envisioned their conversation at all. Ivan was supposed to help him. Adam couldn't understand how he could turn like this. Did Adam really mean nothing to him now that Victor was gone?

Thankfully his words seemed to have sway and Ivan's expression softened further. "Show me," he requested with more gentleness entering his voice than there had been previously.

Adam nodded as hope reignited within him. Of course Ivan had doubts. Why wouldn't he? He would have been told that Adam was a murderer.

But surely if he knew me at all then he wouldn't believe it?

Adam forced away this nagging doubt and took the media capsule from his pocket. He set it down on the desk before turning away. Adam tuned his surroundings out as Ivan picked it up and activated it. He couldn't watch this, not again. He sniffed and reached up to brush tears from his eyes with one hand. Once Ivan had watched the footage he remained silent and it was left up to Adam to speak.

"I didn't mean to do it. Joseph would have…he would have raped me," Adam explained plaintively. Surely Ivan could understand this? He *had* to.

Ivan was oddly quiet as he picked up the media capsule again. His expressions were once more unreadable. Adam forced himself to wait quietly. Ivan was probably shocked by what he had seen. Adam had to give him a few moments. If he pushed him then Ivan might not help him.

"And you've not shown this to anyone else?"

"No," Adam shook his head in confirmation. "Only you."

Ivan remained silent as he dropped the capsule onto the carpet.

"What are you doing?" Adam cried out in utter disbelief as Ivan slammed his foot down on top of it. There was a crunch and the sound of metal breaking. Adam could hardly breathe. He stumbled back slightly, stunned and horrified at what he was witnessing. This couldn't be happening he told himself. Ivan was his godfather. He was supposed to look out for him.

"Climbing the career ladder," Ivan finally answered him. "I've often been criticised for my leniency where you're concerned. Being the arresting officer and charging you with two counts of murder will certainly discard any doubts Jeff Ingham has about my succession."

His career. He cared more about that than he did Adam?

"You…you can't. I didn't mean to do it. I—"

The pretence of being the caring godfather was done away with now. Ivan's face was cold and unfeeling, and Adam felt as though he was addressing a stranger. He really didn't know Ivan at all.

"Who's going to believe you?" Ivan demanded. "You've already got a criminal record and everyone knows how much you hated Joseph Nichols. As far as I'm concerned the case is watertight."

"I'll tell everyone," Adam shot back in desperation. He felt sick. All these years Adam had been lied to by the one person whom he thought was on his side. How could Ivan do this to him?

"No one will believe you. You see in the eyes of the public you're already guilty."

Ivan knew that this was why Adam had come to him. No one else would believe him. Adam was sure that Ivan would also realise that he had made a backup copy of the footage and destroy that too. He wasn't the kind of man who would leave loose ends.

Adam took a step back as Ivan tried to approach him. He

forced his overwhelming disbelief and shock at Ivan's betrayal to one side. He had to get out of here.

Shakily Adam reached under his jacket and produced the gun that he'd taken from Officer Chandra. He'd brought it with him in case he was stopped before he was able to reach Ivan's apartment. However, the thought of actually using it had never crossed his mind. Until now. Ivan hesitated upon seeing the firearm.

"Don't be a fool," he cautioned angrily. "You're already in enough trouble."

What did that matter now? Adam was already guilty and convicted as far as everyone was concerned. At this point he was beyond caring. In his panicked mind all he could think of was getting away.

"I don't want to use this," he warned his godfather. "But I will if I have to."

"No you won't," Ivan shook his head. He was dismissive of Adam's threats as he moved to block the door and Adam's escape. The man was so arrogant that he assumed even now that his relationship with Adam would save him. He was half right. Adam couldn't kill Ivan. He couldn't bear to kill again.

"I just want to leave," Adam replied as he kept the weapon levelled at older man. "Let me and then you can call as many police officers and L.S.A agents as you like. Just give me time to get clear first."

"I can't let you do that."

"Then I don't have a choice."

Ivan cried out at the recoil from the gun and immediately he fell back against the wall as he clutched at his injured right shoulder. Blood began to spread out from the wound, seeping between his fingers and running down the crisp white shirt that he was wearing. But Adam's aim had deliberately been off. Angrily he wiped the tears from his eyes as he approached the injured man.

"You left me with no choice, Ivan," he whispered as he shoved his godfather aside. Adam only paused briefly to collect his computer and eject the media capsule recording the events before fleeing the apartment. He knew that Ivan would have called for backup immediately. But where could he go now? Leaving London was out of the question and Adam had no one else he could turn to. He was completely alone.

CHAPTER FOURTEEN

"I've often been criticised for my leniency where you're concerned. Being the arresting officer and charging you with two counts of murder will certainly discard any doubts Jeff Ingham has about my succession."

His career. He cared more about that than he did Adam?

"You...you can't. I didn't mean to do it. I—"

The pretence of being the caring godfather was done away with now. Ivan's face was cold and unfeeling, and Adam felt as though he was addressing a stranger. He really didn't know Ivan at all.

"Who's going to believe you?" Ivan demanded. "You've already got a criminal record and everyone knows how much you hated Joseph Nichols. As far as I'm concerned the case is watertight."

"I'll tell everyone," Adam shot back in desperation. He felt sick. All these years Adam had been lied to by the one person whom he thought was on his side. How could Ivan do this to him?

"No one will believe you. You see in the eyes of the public you're already guilty."

Adam stood silently; his solitary figure silhouetting the sun's rise against the backdrop of the city skyline. An almost empty bottle of vodka was clutched tightly in his trembling hand. He could not recall just how much he'd had to drink that night. Not that it made any difference. He could still feel it. The agonising weight of his suffering. The loss, hurt and betrayal had consumed him. He did not know how he'd ended up here or even how he'd been able to move around the city without being caught. Caution had left him the moment that he'd fled Ivan's home. He remembered breaking into the kiosk and by some miracle he had been able to make his escape with the alcohol before the police had arrived. Now, however, time and memories had blurred into an indistinguishable mix of sorrow and disillusion. Adam had not wanted any of this.

The bottle slid from his fingertips. Clattering loudly onto New London Bridge it rolled before sliding between the metal railings and into the Thames below. Adam turned and glanced back at the city that had been his home. London had never truly felt like it though. Adam had never belonged there. Or anywhere else. He'd been called a freak. A failure of a science project. And now... Now he was branded a murderer. Adam knew that sooner or later he would be caught. Ivan wouldn't stop until he'd arrested Adam and secured his precious promotion.

I want to change

Adam's words to Ivan at his father's funeral were almost laughable now. He wasn't a killer, but he wasn't far off from becoming one. Now Adam harboured some regrets that he'd not had the stomach to kill the older man. Ivan deserved it.

The way he'd turned on Adam as though his godson meant nothing to him. It was chilling and the depth of betrayal that Adam was feeling was unbearable.

You're always looking out for me, Ivan. You're more of a father to me

Adam uttered a sob as more tears blurred his vision. Without Ivan he had no one. He had no other family or any friends who could help him.

The events of the last few days were a nightmare that Adam could never escape from. He placed his trembling hands on the rail, his fingers tightening around the metal in a bid to steady himself. It didn't have to be like that. Why give Ivan the credit for his arrest? Despite what had happened, when Adam had first fled Venewood he had wanted to escape; he had wanted to live. Now things were different. Ivan would ensure that any future he might have had was taken away from him. Adam had nothing to live for now.

An eerie calm descended upon him as his decision was made. For the first time since Joseph and Eleanor's deaths Adam felt in control. Slowly he climbed up onto the rail.

I just don't like you enough as a person to want to be with you

Adam thought of Leon at that moment. He had loved the blond and Leon had cared nothing for him. Everyone had just been using him.

Vaguely he felt something fall from his jacket and heard it clatter onto the bridge; his computer. It didn't matter if anyone found it or if it was lost with him. Perhaps the footage of what had really happened in Venewood would come to light, but it would be too late for Adam. He could still see Eleanor's terrified expression every time he closed his eyes and Adam just wanted it to stop. He didn't want to feel this much pain and guilt anymore.

The fall was swift and within seconds he had plunged into the river below. The sting of the impact was accompanied by a sharp blow to his left temple. Adam barely had time to register the pain before unconsciousness overcame him.

***

"How could anyone love a son like you?"

"Get off of me! Murderer!"

"You're always looking out for me, Ivan. You're more of a father to me."

"No one will believe you. You see in the eyes of the public you're already guilty."

"I just don't like you enough as a person to want to be with you."

"I want to change."

Adam gasped as he sat up in bed. He was immediately assaulted by some momentary dizziness and he squeezed his eyes shut again. He kept them closed until it had worn off. Adam's throat felt dry and he swallowed a couple of times in a bid to relieve himself of this feeling. His entire body was trembling and he could feel the wet of tears on his cheeks. Slowly he reached up with a hand and wiped the damp away. Only then did he pay attention to his surroundings. He was home in his bed at Venewood. Adam looked round the room in confusion. How had he got back here? The last thing he recalled was climbing up onto New London Bridge. How had he made it home?

Tentatively Adam got up. He was dressed in a pair of

white cotton trousers and a long-sleeved white shirt; these were a far cry from his usually choice of attire. This further alarmed him. The brilliant white of the fabric hurt his eyes. In fact the entire contrast of the room seemed unnecessarily bright and Adam's eyes failed to adjust even as seconds stretched into minutes. It wasn't completely unbearable and he decided to do his best to ignore it. He walked over to his door and nervously pressed the tile to open it. As Adam went through he noticed that the open hallway seemed to be just as bright. He didn't understand what was going on. Why was he here? Why hadn't he died?

"I don't care if it takes you the rest of the day, I want everything up and running by this evening," a painfully familiar voice floated down the hallway. Adam gasped. There had to be some mistake. It couldn't be…his line of thought trailed off as Adam broke into a run. He raced down the hallway and to his father's office. The door was open and Victor glanced up in annoyance as Adam rushed into the room.

"I'll call you back," he told whoever it was he was speaking to. He ended the call and glared at his son.

"What do you want now, Adam?" he demanded. Victor was sitting behind his desk and the inbuilt computer screen was scrolling a combination of numbers and letters. He pressed the standby button in the corner of the screen when he realised that his son's gaze was on it. He was wearing the clothes that Adam had last seen him in; one of his burgundy suits.

"You…you're…" Adam broke off as immense relief of the obvious flooded him. A dream. It had all been a horrible dream.

"What is it?" Victor continued irately as he stood up. "I am in the middle of working on some very important projects. What on Earth is so important that you felt the need to interrupt me in such a dramatic fashion?"

"I…I just…it's so good to see you," Adam blurted as his emotions got the better of him. Despite their differences Adam had never felt happier to see the older man. His father frowned; he was clearly taken aback by Adam's outburst. "Have you been drinking again?"

"Is that where I was last night?" Adam asked softly. "Did Ivan bring me home again?" He wasn't overly concerned with his whereabouts, but a part of him was still unsettled for reasons that Adam couldn't pinpoint.

"I don't know what you're talking about," Victor snapped. "Now is there something you wanted?"

Father...I hate things being like this between us, don't you?

Adam recalled their conversation on the night of the party. At that point he had given up hope, but his nightmare was too raw for him to dismiss easily. He had another chance and Adam was going to take it.

"I'm sorry," Adam rushed out. "I'm so sorry for everything."

His father did not respond verbally at first. His stern expression faded and was replaced with a look that Adam did not immediately recognise having not ever seen his father react this way before. It was a look of regret. He turned away and went over to the window. He kept his back to Adam as he spoke. "I'm sorry too, Adam."

Adam's shoulders slumped as he released a breath that he didn't realise he had been holding. "I'm going to get help," he added. “Maybe see one of those doctors that Ivan mentioned. I want to change. I want us to have a better relationship.”

“It’s too late for that, Adam,” Victor responded gravely. “Far too late.”

“It isn’t. Not if we both—”

“Look what you did!” Victor cut him off sharply.

Adam glanced down and a cry lodged itself in his throat. Joseph lay on the carpet. He was on his back, his eyes staring lifelessly up at the ceiling. There was a pool of blood around his head and the right side of his temple had been almost completely crushed inwards. The statue of Plutus lay discarded beside the body. Adam felt sick when his gaze lingered on it and he saw fragments of bone and hair sticking to the bloodied edge of the ornament.

“I…” Adam trailed off as memories of his nightmare began to surface. Yet it hadn’t been a nightmare; he was now in one. “I didn’t mean to kill him. He was going to…he was going to rape me,” his words echoed those that he had spoken to Ivan. That had been real. This…this wasn’t reality. It was so much worse than that.

At these words Victor moved. He whirled around and within two seconds he was at Adam’s side. Adam cried out when his father seized him painfully by the shoulders and shook him.

“Don’t lie to me! Joseph would never do anything like that! You murdered them because you didn’t inherit my fortune!” The lambent fury in his father’s voice was intermingled with pain for the loss of his family. Adam was used to the anger, to the disappointment, but the additional grief was unbearable. Adam cringed as he looked away.

"Father," he forced himself to speak, to start pleading as Victor began to drag him from the room. "It was an accident, I didn't mean—"

He broke off when his father shoved him roughly to the edge of the stairs. Looking down over the rail Adam saw Eleanor's body. She lay in a heap at the bottom step. Her hair had come free from its usual bun. The blonde strands were stained with crimson rivets, darker and thicker at the top of her head before thinning out as they ran down the stray locks. There wasn't as much blood as there was with Joseph, but Adam knew that she was dead. He had killed her. He remembered that.

"You killed all of us," his father said furiously. "Your selfish rebellion drove me into an early grave."

"No!" Adam pleaded. "I never…I didn't mean…"

"But you did. You knew I was unwell and still you kept pushing. Further and further until your disgusting antics with that lowlife from the poor sector finally finished me off. It is your fault I'm dead!"

"Father—"

"Shut up!"

The sharp blow to Adam's face silenced him. He fell back against the rail that had previously been supporting him. He whimpered as he glanced back out over the reception foyer. A third body near to the door left Adam feeling cold.

"Father…" he asked in a choked whisper. "Who is that?"

"His death was the only good thing to come out of any of this. Imagine if he'd have told anyone about the two of you. The Larimore family name would have been ruined if it had gotten out that you shared another man's bed!"

"Leon!" Adam cried out as the identity of the third body

suddenly became clear. He pushed his father aside and raced down the stairs. He almost tripped over Eleanor's body at the bottom and he was not mindful of kicking it as he ran to his lover's side. Adam crashed to his knees beside his lover. Leon was dead. As Adam gently rolled him over onto his back he saw ugly blue and purple bruising around his neck. It looked as though he had been strangled.

You kind of act like a spoilt brat most of the time. You're completely self-obsessed and let's face it, even though you say you hate the idea that you were genetically engineered for a single purpose, you think you're so much better than everyone else. I don't think you care about me. I don't think you care about anyone other than yourself

"When you've already done it once it's easier to do it again," Victor leaned down and murmured in Adam's ear. Adam had been so focused on Leon that he hadn't heard his father's approach. "You didn't like the nasty things he was saying about you. They were a little close to home weren't they? Then he made it clear that he was using you and that pushed you over the edge. After you'd killed your family you went back there. What was one more? That was your reasoning and Leon deserved it. He had made a fool of you. Used you."

"No!" Adam vehemently denied. "I haven't seen Leon since we argued!"

"Really?" Victor questioned. "Is that the truth or is it what you want to believe?"

"No!" Adam cried out as he leapt to his feet. As he released Leon's body it fell back onto the floor. The lifeless eyes that stared accusingly up at Adam was more than he could take.

"You killed all of them!" Victor snarled out as he blocked Adam's escape.

"I didn't mean to," Adam pleaded brokenly as he found himself backed into the front door. "Father..."

He gagged as a hand closed around his throat. His father lifted him almost effortlessly and pinned him back against the metal. Adam flailed, desperately clawing at the hand that held him, but it was no use; he couldn't break free of the grip his father had on him.

"Father—" Adam choked out as his vision began to rapidly darken. The last thing he was aware of was Victor's cold gaze as everything went black.

***

Adam cried out as he was torn from unconsciousness. He bolted up right, his wild gaze roaming the strange room that he found himself in. Almost immediately panic and vertigo slammed into him. He doubled over, vomiting a disgusting combination of vodka and acid over the side of the bed. He shuddered, wrapping his arms around himself as his body shook from the sudden effort and the terror of his still vivid nightmare. But it hadn't all been a dream. Tears wet his cheeks as the reality of his situation threatened to overwhelm him. Adam drew a racking sob as he recalled his fall from the bridge and the events leading up to it.

I wish I'd died...

Adam sobbed harder as he processed this thought. He didn't want to be here. It would have been better if his suicide attempt had been successful. Adam would be better off dead.

"How could anyone love a son like you?"

"Get off of me! Murderer!"

"You're always looking out for me, Ivan. You're more of a father to me."

"No one will believe you. You see in the eyes of the public you're already guilty."

"I just don't like you enough as a person to want to be with you."

"I want to change."

Echoes of conversations, events and betrayals swirled to the forefront of Adam's mind until he could hardly bear it. He leapt up off of the bed. This action caused the room to spin even faster. His feet slid in his own vomit and Adam crashed painfully to the floor. He gasped as the breath was knocked from his body upon his impact. Before he could right himself he suddenly felt someone at his side. Adam lashed out, roughly shoving the other person away from him. He scrambled across the floor, only getting as far as the end of the bed before he felt hands seize him by his shoulders.

"No!" Adam cried out in utter terror as he found himself wrestled to the floor. In his weakened state he was unable to effectively fight back and so he was quickly pinned back against the carpet.

"Mr Larimore!" the female voice above him called urgently. "Please don't struggle. I'm not going to hurt you."

Adam sobbed when he felt a sharp scratch of a needle. Moments later the colour began to drain from the room. Adam's vision started to darken at the edges, moving steadily inward until all he could see was black. He was vaguely aware of a figure leaning over him before his consciousness faded once more.

CHAPTER FIFTEEN

When Adam next became aware of his surroundings it was evening again. He was once more lying in the single bed with a sheet pulled over him. Adam expected to feel sick or at least experience some kind of pain, but thanks to his regenerative capabilities any discomfort that he should have been feeling had left him as he slept. Carefully Adam drew the sheet back and stared at the white gown he was wearing; it was not that dissimilar to the one he had worn in the hospital. This increased Adam's confusion and panic. What was going on? Where was he?

Adam looked around, taking in his surroundings for the first time. The apartment itself was open plan with the single bed in one corner nearest to the smaller of the two windows. There was another larger window in the left wall with a light brown, two-seater sofa underneath it. A metal coffee table stood in front of it. There were a couple of digital photo frames on the wall showing an elderly couple. The man in the pictures appeared European in origin. The kitchen was on the opposite side of the room. There were four metal counters with a sink in the one on the end. At the other end was a fridge-freezer and free-standing oven as well as a small circular table with a couple of chairs set around it. The apartment was lit by lamps mounted onto the walls.

By Adam's standards the apartment was very cramped, but it was luxury living compared to many other homes in London. This told him that his rescuer must have a decent job at least. Rescuer? Was that what she was? Then why had she drugged him?

I'm not going to hurt you

He could not trust the assurance of a stranger, not when those closest to him had betrayed him. Adam was certain that the police would be offering some kind of reward for information that led to his arrest. What if she intended on handing him over? What if that had been why she had drugged him? He ought to get away now whilst he still could.

Adam tentatively sat up and swung both legs over the side of the bed. Thankfully any other injuries that he might have sustained as a result of his fall into the Thames seemed to have healed.

Adam froze as he recalled once more the events that had brought him here. He had tried to kill himself. He had thrown himself from the bridge with the intention of ending his life. He swallowed hard as he felt himself begin to shake. He'd come so close…Adam slumped forward in despair. His father…Leon…Joseph…Eleanor…Ivan's betrayal. Of all that had happened the latter hurt just as badly.

Do you also realise that my obligation to you ended when your father, my closest friend, died?

The man whom had been a father figure as far as Adam

was concerned had cast him aside without a thought. Ivan was just like Victor; he only cared for his career and for the power that it gave him. Adam curled his hands into fists as the anger, that for the last couple of days had been muted, returned. His father, Leon and now Ivan…everyone who ought to have cared for him had only seen him as an object, someone to be used to their advantage. Victor Larimore hadn't wanted a son, he had just wanted his name to live on after he died. Leon hadn't cared about Adam; he'd just wanted a fling and Adam could have been anyone.

You didn't like the nasty things he was saying about you. They were a little close to home weren't they? Then he made it clear he was using you and that pushed you over the edge. After you'd killed your family you went back there. What was one more? That was your reasoning and Leon deserved it. He had made a fool of you. Used you.

Adam flinched as he recalled that terrible dream. Had he killed Leon? Had he really gone back there? The events of the last few days had blurred and there were gaps. What if he—No! Adam cut this line of thought off before it could manifest itself. He had not hurt Leon. He couldn't have done that, despite what the blond had done to him.

Once more Adam's thoughts turned to Ivan. Ivan who had the power to ensure that Adam was treated fairly and not locked up for two counts of murder. Ivan could have helped Adam and ended this nightmare. Instead he had chosen to betray his godson in order to gain his promotion.

I wish I'd died…

Adam recalled his earlier thoughts and, as he allowed his anger to take hold, he realised that he no longer wanted to die; he wanted revenge. Ivan was going to pay dearly for his betrayal.

Adam wasn't entirely sure where he was going to go, but he had to try and make it out of London. If he could manage that then he could seek refuge in one of the other cities and formulate his plan. Tentatively Adam tried to stand. As he did so felt a rush of momentary weakness, although thankfully it passed within seconds. Adam spotted his own clothes neatly folded up on top of the coffee table. They had been cleaned and were dry. Adam pulled them on and then hurried towards the door. It was locked although the standard mechanism for the inside meant that pressing a single icon on the LCD screen would open the door. The sign on the opposite side of the corridor told Adam that he was on the second floor. He couldn't hear anyone about and so he decided to chance it. Adam made his way down the hall. His heart was thumping almost painfully in his chest. This was almost riskier than going out onto the streets. If he was spotted inside the apartment block there was a limitation on where he could go. At least outside he could make a proper break for it.

He still felt weak and Adam was aware that his progress was almost painfully slow because of this. He kept one hand pressed against the wall as he walked. Just carry on, Adam told himself. *Don't think about how you're feeling, just keep on going.*

Adam froze when he suddenly heard footsteps approaching from the other end of the corridor. He glanced around but there was nowhere to go.

"Mr Larimore?" a voice softly called his name. It wasn't the shout of recognition that Adam had been expecting. He glanced up and immediately realised that he knew the woman approaching.

"Dr Ramirez?"

"Carla," she corrected him kindly.

"You're the one who saved me?" he realised and her nod confirmed this.

"Please come back inside before someone sees you." She was carrying a bag and had clearly been out of the apartment block. Carla had taken a chance leaving him here alone. Why would she do that?

The desire to find out was tempting, but to linger here too long was dangerous and so Adam reluctantly shook his head. "I have to leave the city."

"You're not in a fit state to go anywhere," Carla told him worriedly. "And you sustained quite a nasty head injury when you fell. You need to rest."

Adam bit his lip; he wanted to believe her but why would she help him? Why would anyone when there was more than likely a substantial reward for information leading to his arrest?

"You drugged me," he reminded her. "Why should I believe that you want to help me?"

"You were making a lot of noise. I was worried that you would be discovered or that you would hurt yourself. I don't blame you for not trusting me, but if I had wanted to turn you in I would have done it whilst you were unconscious. You'll barely make it out of the apartment block in your current state. Please, Mr Larimore."

Adam didn't know what to think or whether or not he should believe her. However, Carla was right about one thing. Just standing was taxing his strength and Adam was starting to feel faint. Tentatively, and as though to test himself, he removed his hands from the wall and took a couple of steps.

The corridor started to spin and he felt Carla reach out to steady him. She was right; he wasn't going to get very far at all like this. It wasn't a case of trusting her; Adam had no choice. He nodded quickly and offered no protest as she wrapped an arm around his shoulders and started to lead him back to her apartment. Once they were inside Carla insisted that Adam lay back down. He did so, albeit grudgingly, and immediately started to question her, much to the doctor's obvious exasperation.

"What happened?" he asked her. "Why did you save me?"

"I was walking to work and I saw you jump," she answered reluctantly. "Why don't you get some sleep? You don't have to worry, I'm not going to turn you in, Mr Larimore."

"Adam," he murmured, "and I don't know that. You might have saved me for the reward money."

"Then why would I go to all this trouble?" she countered with some frustration at Adam's continued accusations. "I could have just dragged you from the river and called the police."

"True," Adam admitted reluctantly. "So why didn't you?"

Carla sighed in annoyance. "You're not going to get any sleep until I explain, are you?"

"No," Adam answered firmly.

"I'll tell you and then you must promise you will get some rest."

"If I'm satisfied you've told me the truth." Adam knew how ungrateful he sounded, but he was wary about trusting anyone. Everyone he'd ever placed any kind of faith in had betrayed him. Why should he trust Carla, a complete stranger?

"I didn't think you'd wake up for another couple of

hours," Carla admitted. "So I went to the kiosk on the next street. If you won't sleep will you at least eat something? Then we can talk about why I'm helping you."

"Okay," Adam agreed. Now that he thought about it he was slightly hungry. He couldn't remember when he had last eaten something. His agreement seemed to please Carla anyway and she hurried over to the kitchen area to make him something. She returned a few minutes later with two slices of toast with honey on them. Adam accepted the plate with thanks, however, despite his grumbling stomach he was more interested in what Carla had to say and prompted her to continue.

Carla sat down on the edge of the bed. "I saved you because I'm a doctor. I've devoted my life to helping people. It doesn't matter who they are or what they've done. After I pulled you from the river I managed to get you back here without being seen. You'd hit your head, but apart from that you were unhurt. I stitched up your wound and changed your clothes. I found a computer and a media capsule on the bridge. I'm assuming they are yours?"

"Yeah they are. Are you going to hand me over to the police?"

"The news story on the Information Bank says that you murdered Joseph Nichols and Eleanor Larimore, and that you then attacked the first police officer to attend the scene."

"It was an accident," Adam murmured. It took him a while, but he was able to explain to Carla what had really happened. She sat down on the corner of the bed and listened in silence. She never said a word, even when Adam faltered in places that were painful to speak about. When he had finished he found himself close to tears again.

"I believe you," she said without hesitation.

"Why? Why would you?"

Carla smiled and reached out to touch his hand. "I've treated many people including murderers. You can tell that they are guilty just by looking into their eyes. There's a coldness there, an unfeeling that makes them capable of deliberately and brutally taking the life of another. I do not see that in your eyes. I know it was an accident."

Adam didn't know what to say to this. So many people had lied to him, used him. Why was she any different? "I have the security footage of all of it on my computer. Don't you want to see it for yourself before trusting what I've said?"

"Would you like me to?"

Adam shrugged. "You've said you believe me, but if you want proof that I'm telling the truth then it's on there."

"I will watch it if you feel you want me to," Carla reluctantly agreed. "Now I would advise you to get some rest. I'm not going to turn you in and you can stay here for as long as you need to."

"Thank you. I…" he trailed off, not knowing what else to say.

"Mr Larimore?" Carla ventured when the silence dragged on for too long. "I'm not that kind of doctor, but if you need to talk to someone—"

"No, thank you," Adam cut her off as politely as he could. He didn't want to talk about it. He was too angry and the deaths were still too raw.

Carla seemed to understand this. She remained seated on the bed until Adam had eaten.

"I had to reschedule my shift at the hospital," Carla said as she took the empty plate from Adam. "I'll be there until midday tomorrow. If you want anything please help yourself."

"Thank you."

Carla smiled. "You don't need to thank me. Please get some rest. I'll see you tomorrow afternoon."

She left and went through to the bathroom to start getting ready for work. Adam lay back down and closed his eyes. He did not go to sleep. A part of him still felt very much in shock. In the space of a few weeks his life had turned into a nightmare. A nightmare where there was no escape. Adam swallowed hard in a bid to fight back his upset. He had to get a hold of himself. Becoming a victim wouldn't help him. He needed to be strong and focus on making Ivan pay.

Even though Carla seemed like a good person Adam still couldn't shake the feeling that there was another reason that she was helping him. This would be revealed sooner or later, he was sure. For now he was certain that he could trust that she would not turn him in. With this in mind Adam decided that he would wait until he was feeling more or less recovered and then he would leave. Then he would begin to plan his revenge. Adam actually regretted not killing Ivan when he'd had the chance, but death was the least that the man deserved. Adam was going to take everything from him; let him know what it felt like to lose all that he'd worked for. Adam would take great pleasure in destroying the older man.

CHAPTER SIXTEEN

When you've already done it once it's easier to do it again. You didn't like the nasty things he was saying about you. They were a little close to home weren't they? Then he made it clear he was using you and that pushed you over the edge. After you'd killed your family you went back there. What was one more? That was your reasoning and Leon deserved it. He had made a fool of you. Used you

Adam gasped as he bolted up in bed. He was breathing hard as his hands clutched the sheet at his chest. His forehead was coated in a light sheen of sweat and he felt a droplet run a path down his brow.

Leon…

It wasn't true…he repeated over and over as he forced himself to hold onto the resolve that he had not harmed his ex-lover; the resolve that he had felt yesterday. Yet the reoccurrence of that dream made those tiny doubts in the back of his mind seem magnified. Adam swallowed hard and shifted so that he was leaning back against the headboard. He would never have hurt Leon, Adam told himself over and over.

Just like you would never have hurt Eleanor...those nasty little thoughts reminded him mockingly. You don't know what you're capable of...

Adam drew a sharp breath as his gaze flitted to his computer sitting on the bedside cabinet. He leaned over and retrieved it. He'd left it on so that Carla could view the security footage when she got home. As much as Adam didn't want anyone to see it he knew it was the only way to reassure himself that he could place his trust in her; even if she did have some ulterior motive for helping him.

The computer had been connected to the communal Internet for the apartment block and with a small adjustment Adam was able to make the connection secure. The last thing he wanted was his call being traced. Then with trepidation he pressed the 'phone' icon next to Leon's name in his video contacts list.

It rang for at least five minutes before automatically disconnecting. Adam tried again and again, but Leon wasn't answering. Finally he sent an instant message to Leon's account asking him to just let Adam know that he was all right. Leon would view it a strange request if he was considering how they had left things. Adam then logged into the Information Bank and ran a quick search for deaths within the city in the last few days. Much to his relief Leon's name wasn't listed. Feeling more relaxed, Adam was about to close the browser down when a 'breaking news' icon flashed in an indication that a new and important story had just been uploaded. Adam immediately pressed the square to open the news article.

IVAN WILLIAMS FORMALLY ANNOUNCED AS THE NEW HEAD OF THE L.S.A

In a publicity event this morning the current Head of the L.S.A Jeff Ingham formally confirmed that he would be stepping down within the next year. Jeff Ingham also announced Chief of Police Ivan Williams as his successor. Ivan Williams is a former General of the Army with over twenty five years of experience, fifteen of which were at senior level. Ivan left the army in 2110 after he was injured during a confrontation with Scottish militants. Once he was recovered, Ivan took up his current position as Chief of Police and under his direction crime within the city has reduced by thirty percent.

"I am absolutely delighted by Jeff Ingham's decision," Ivan Williams was quoted saying. "For many years I have dedicated my life to ensuring that our laws are upheld for the safety of London's citizens. I am greatly honoured to be given the opportunity to continue to ensure the safety and security of our great nation through my new position. I am also very excited for the opportunity to work with Eric Rawlins, a man who's tireless and selfless efforts far surpass my own accomplishments."

Ivan Williams is the youngest man to be appointed Head of the L.S.A and his exceptional achievements in both his previous position and during his life in the military are guarantees that London and the rest of England are in very safe and experienced hands.

Adam scoffed in disgust as he read the article. He knew that Ivan talked a good talk, but it was sickening to read how he pretended that all he cared about was England's interests and that he used Eric Rawlins in a charade of false modesty.

The only thing Ivan cared about was himself. As far as Adam was concerned this crushed any remnants of feeling he had towards his godfather. Ivan had now achieved all that he wanted whilst Adam had lost everything.

The rest of the day went by quicker than Adam had been expecting. He'd slept for some of it, albeit fitfully. He could only manage a few hours before the nightmares took hold again. Whilst some people might say that they would fade in time Adam did not believe it would be the case for him. And a part of him did not want them to. If he was caught he would be imprisoned, most likely for life, but as far as Adam was concerned he was already carrying out a life sentence.

Adam had logged back into the Information Bank later on and saw that the reward for information leading to his capture had gone up to five figures. Adam was somewhat disdainful of this. Ten thousand pounds was still a rather meagre amount considering the combined Larimore and Nichols' fortunes.

He glanced up as the door to the apartment slid open. Carla had clearly been delayed as it was now early evening. The doctor smiled tiredly as she entered the room. She was carrying a paper bag in addition to her handbag and set this down in the kitchen before making her way over the bed.

"How are you feeling?"

"Much better, thank you," Adam answered. "How was work?"

"Busy. There was an accidental release of Sevoflurane at one of the Nuclear Control Centres."

Sevoflurane was an anaesthetic gas, which was often used in Government defence systems. If the building that it was used in became compromised or under attack then the gas would be released. Usually the dosage would render people unconscious, but judging from Carla's expression it was much more serious.

"Were there fatalities?" Adam asked.

"Three," Carla sighed. "I wish they wouldn't use anaesthetics in that way. There was very little I could do for them."

"I'm sure you did what you could."

She forced a smile. "That's kind of you, Mr Larimore."

"Adam," he corrected her with a sigh. "I saw that Ivan got his promotion. I hope he enjoys it whilst it lasts!"

Carla frowned although she chose not comment on Adam's remark. "I didn't feel like cooking," she said as she went back to the kitchen area. "So I bought us both a takeaway. I wasn't sure what you'd like so I got a couple of options. We can reheat what we don't eat now for tomorrow."

"I'm not fussy or anything," Adam replied dismissively. He hadn't given eating much thought if he was honest. He'd rather start planning how he was going to make Ivan's life more difficult.

Carla sensed that he wasn't that hungry and plated up the takeaway in silence. She was rather insistent that Adam joined her at the small table to eat. Adam reluctantly agreed. He didn't want to upset her as she was risking so much already by helping him.

The takeaway consisted of several small components that made up the entire meal. There was chicken coated in breadcrumbs, a selection of vegetables in this case mushrooms, sweetcorn and peas, and potatoes with an herb dressing. In the past takeaways had been quite unhealthy, but in modern times all kiosks selling them had to adhere to dietary guidelines set out by the Government's Health and

Lifestyle department. There was also a side salad provided free of charge and a glass bottle of water. The pudding was a small slice of raspberry cheesecake.

They made small talk whilst eating. Carla told Adam more about her shift at the hospital. Then as they started the desserts Carla asked Adam if he'd given much thought into what he was going to do.

Adam hesitated before answering. He doubted that saying that he planned revenge would sit well with her. "Leave the city I guess. Staying here is too dangerous for me." This was the truth and Adam did want to leave London; he didn't know how he was going to achieve this. All the defence posts were manned and he wasn't exactly inconspicuous.

"Mr Larimore," Carla began, suddenly becoming nervous. "There is something I'd like to talk to you about."

"What is it?" Adam asked as he felt himself tensing.

"I know someone who can help you, but what I have to say may shock you."

Adam chuckled inwardly at this. After all he'd been through he doubted that she could say anything that might surprise him. However, he did not voice these thoughts and waited in silence for her to continue.

"You're not the first person on the wrong side of the law whom I have helped. Do you remember the attack on the L.H.A.G.S a couple of years ago?"

Adam nodded. How could he not? Terrorists, believed to be Scottish in origin, had managed to get through security on the outskirts of London and had planted a bomb at the hospital. Thirty people had been killed including the terrorists. Since the war the relationship between Scotland and England had broken down and there were occasionally skirmishes.

Scotland was a lot worse off since England cut all ties with the former nations of the United Kingdom. They had trouble producing enough food and did not have many of the technological advancements that people in England took for granted. The attacks were believed to be organised by the Scottish Government, although they had denied involvement when confronted. Resentment had led to these attacks and since then Adam was often hearing of how the L.S.A had foiled attacks on London and London interests.

"I was working at the accident and emergency unit at the Ralph Gunner Memorial Hospital," Carla continued. Ralph Gunner had been the first Prime Minister after the Great Tsunamis. His leadership and major drive in Government-funded technology was credited with saving the country from ruin. He was a celebrated leadership figure and one that all future Prime Ministers had strived to emulate.

"I was treating the injured who were brought in," Carla added. "There was one man whom we were having trouble finding records for. My scanner read his fingerprints but they didn't match the name he had given me."

Fingerprint scanners had been introduced at all hospitals about fifteen years ago to quickly identify the injured and also alert the police if wanted criminals were brought in for treatment.

"I'd never encountered this before and I didn't know quite what to do. I had my suspicions that perhaps he had been involved in the attack. Ivan Williams was working with Jeff Ingham on the investigation and he had just arrived at the hospital to question those who had only sustained minor injuries. I was going to report the matter to him, but then I received a visit from Dale Jacobs."

Thirty-five year old Dale Jacobs was the Head of the Health and Lifestyle department. Adam had met him briefly when he had been installing some software in their offices in Sector Four. He'd seemed quite a go getter who had shown much more interest in Adam's programming skills than most. In fact, Adam seemed to recall he had to charge them an extra couple of hours as Jacobs had asked so many questions.

"Dale identified the man as a member of his team and asked me to patch him up as soon as possible before releasing him into Dale's care. I thought this was rather odd as Dale implied that he was a junior team member and certainly not someone whom a senior official would usually take the trouble to check up on. I queried the fact that the man wasn't in the database and Dale said that the system had been having some problems. Something told me that he wasn't being entirely truthful as officials from Dale's department were rarely at the L.H.A.G.S. He stayed until I had completed the computerised identification. The injured man seemed on edge as though he was worried that I would report him. I was considering it and Dale must have realised as he was waiting for me outside the cubicle once I'd finished tending to the man. He requested that I accompany him to one of the offices down the hall. Looking back I should have been more concerned for my safety than I was at the time and been less willing to go with him. As it was a crowded hospital full of police and L.S.A agents I felt more secure about the situation than I would have done normally. Once we were alone Dale confirmed that the man had been part of the group who had attacked the L.H.A.G.S. My first reaction was that I should report him, after all he had just murdered twenty-three L.S.A employees and three civilians, but there was something in his voice that made me hesitate.

He gave me a rather ancient looking portable computer; it was probably about ten years out of date at least. He told me to view the files marked 'Genetics' and then I was free to call the L.S.A if I wished," Carla laughed sadly and shook her head. "I don't know what I thought I would read in those files, but it certainly wasn't what was there."

"The files told you about the Government and L.S.A genetics programme didn't they?" Adam guessed softly.

Carla's eyes widened in surprise. "How do you know about that?"

"Ivan offered me a job with the L.S.A once he was promoted. I hacked their system out of curiosity. My computer is full of their dirty little secrets."

"It's appalling isn't it," she said softly. "Every time a person is admitted to hospital suffering from cancer or another terminal illness I look at them and wonder if they had been genetically engineered to die, especially when they're from a less affluent family. Dale told me that they attacked the hospital because they don't believe in the genetics programme. In Scotland women are still free to conceive naturally, although there is a one child limit due to resources being restricted. Dale said that it is a harder life there, but a free one."

"Did Dale explain why he's helping them?" Adam asked. This certainly was interesting and he was curious to learn how it was going to link to his current situation.

"He has Scottish heritage and he also doesn't believe in how the Government and L.S.A run England. He wants to change some things back to how they were before the Great Tsunamis. Many people feel that even though the past is a mistake to be learned from there were some aspects of life back then that were better."

Adam agreed with that. The reason he was so drawn to the pre-disaster England was the freedom that everyone had and the diversity of life. Now everything was the same; regimented and boring.

"Dale's been leading a double life as a Scottish agent for nearly ten years now. He's perfectly placed to provide their Government with information, mainly technological to assist with Scotland catching up. As you know a lot of the technology we take for granted now was based on pre-war developments that had been used previously only for Government or military operations. There were tensions between England and Scotland even before so they were deliberately held back."

"But the genetics programme is the reason that you agreed to help him?"

Carla nodded. "As a doctor I've seen so much suffering. All that pain and misery caused by our own Government. They have been lying to us since the war. This is not the perfect world that they would have us believe. Life is only better if you're a high up member of the L.S.A, part of the Government or from a rich family. The Government say that they are trying to make life better for everyone, but all they are interested in is control. The genetics programme was supposed to help people, not sentence them to death. I've been developing existing technology that could help fight cancer. I have plans for a machine that can use the laser technology from the defence shields to vaporise foreign bodies, for example bullets, without the need for intrusive and potentially life-threatening surgery. It could also be developed further to remove tumours. I've applied to the Government's medial department for funding, but they've rejected my application for a grant three times. They've said that the technology isn't viable. Now I know why. They are not interested in helping normal people."

"They only care about power," Adam agreed, "and Ivan is the same. Nothing will change now he's been made Head of the L.S.A."

"Dale offered me to the chance to go to Scotland, but England is my home. I don't want to abandon it. So I help him where I can; mainly patching up his operatives if they're hurt. I have a secure line to contact him on. I believe he may be able to help you, Mr Larimore."

Adam remained silent for a moment as suddenly her motives became clear.

"No. You think I might be able to help them," he corrected her. "That's why you pulled me from the river."

"I meant what I said; I do want to help you. I thought that you could request asylum in Scotland in return for your computer expertise. They desperately need help and you are the best in your field. It is an opportunity that I couldn't let go by."

"And what if Dale Jacobs decides to turn me in for the reward money instead?" Adam asked hesitantly. He was loath to trust any Government official even one who was allegedly leading a double life.

"He won't. Dale will see the same opportunities for both of you that I do. Let me call him."

Adam took some time to consider his options. He didn't have many. He couldn't stay with Carla forever so the alternatives were that he could try to get out of the city on his own or he could trust Dale Jacobs. Adam doubted that he would get very far on his own. Every L.S.A agent and police officer in London would be looking for him. He had been lucky to make it as far as he had. If Carla was wrong about Dale Jacobs then Adam was going to be arrested. But she did seem very sure of the man and even though she had ulterior motives for helping Adam, these had come from a desire to help people. This was the only reason that Adam hadn't become angry with her. Carla genuinely wanted to help England and she'd not harmed Adam or threatened to turn him in. She was offering him an opportunity.

"Okay," Adam nodded in agreement after a few minutes. "Call him."

"You're making the right decision," she told him. "Dale will help you. I think due to this I ought to watch the security footage from Venewood. Of course I believe you and it might help if I could show it to Dale too."

"No," Adam shook his head. It was difficult enough for him to let Carla view it; he was reluctant to let anyone else see what had happened. It wasn't so much the deaths, but Joseph's attack; the idea of a stranger seeing that made Adam uncomfortable.

Carla appeared to sense this and let the matter drop. If they really wanted Adam's help to advance Scotland's computer systems then he doubted that Dale Jacobs would be too interested in whether or not he was a murderer anyway.

Murderer… Adam shuddered and forced his darkening thoughts to one side.

"I know it's early, but I think I'm going to get some sleep. Can you set the meeting up for tomorrow?"

Carla nodded. "Are you all right?"

"Fine," Adam assured her with more conviction than he

felt inside. “I just feel rather tired.” This was a lie; Adam knew that he wouldn’t be able to sleep well, he just didn’t want to continue the conversation.

As the entire living space was open plan Carla busied herself in the kitchen cleaning up the plates whilst he got ready for bed. Carla had bought him some black pyjamas to replace the gown from the hospital that he had been wearing. Adam felt bad taking the only bed for another night and so he moved to the sofa. Carla protested at this when she turned back around to face the room, but Adam insisted. They didn’t talk again. After a few minutes Carla moved over to the bed and collected Adam’s computer from the bedside cabinet. She went into the bathroom to the view the footage. Adam closed his eyes as he heard it beginning and he actually willed sleep to come quickly to him. He didn’t want to ever see or hear that footage again.

As Adam finally drifted off he did so hoping that he’d done the right thing.

CHAPTER SEVENTEEN

Dale Jacobs did not arrive until late afternoon. As a senior Government official he couldn't simply drop everything and not offer an explanation as to why. He entered the apartment without needing Carla to open the door for him. Adam wasn't really surprised that she had added his thumbprint to the security program. It was quite obvious from the way she looked at Jacobs that she was in love with him.

Adam remained seated on the sofa as Jacobs greeted him; he shook the man's hand before lounging back against the cushions. He was certain that he appeared more confident than he was feeling and hoped that this wrong-footed Jacobs. He didn't want to give the impression that he was as anxious as he felt.

"Adam," Jacobs started in a typically formal and official fashion as he sat down next to him. "Carla has filled me in on what has happened, but perhaps you would be so kind as to tell me in your own words?"

Adam shrugged nonchalantly. "There's not a lot to tell

really. I killed my stepbrother in self-defence and when my stepmother found us I accidently pushed her down the stairs. I tried going to Ivan Williams for help, but he'd rather screw me over and get a promotion than do the right thing."

Jacobs appeared almost as taken aback as Carla at this new found attitude. Adam on the other hand found it quite comforting. It was easier to talk flippantly about matters that pained him. It made Adam feel detached from what he'd done…almost.

Jacobs sighed and cast a glance in Carla's direction. His clean-cut, office boy looks didn't exactly make him stand out as a double agent, Adam mused to himself as he took the break in conversation as an opportunity to study the older man. He was tall, about six foot three or four, with very dark brown almost black hair that was cut to just below his ears. His eyes were blue-green and the slightly wide set of them gave him a trustful look about him. However, Adam knew better than to make assumptions about people based on their looks; he himself was proof of this.

"Carla told me that she saved your life and that you wish to leave the city," Jacobs began when it became apparent that Adam had little to add to what had already been said. "I believe that I can be some assistance in the matter. However, there are—" he broke off when the inbuilt phone on Carla's portable computer began to ring. She apologised and answered it. Her conversation was short and somewhat hurried.

"One of my colleagues has called in sick," she explained apologetically. "So they've asked me to go in early. I'll be back as soon as I can."

The two men sat in silence until Carla was ready to leave. She said a rather lengthy goodbye to Jacobs and told Adam that she would see him later. Once she had left, however, the façade was dropped.

"So then," Jacobs started, "now we're alone I think we can start talking honestly, don't you, Adam?"

Adam tensed. "You knew she was going to get called away, didn't you?"

He smiled somewhat slyly. "I arranged it. I'd rather we spoke privately."

"You're not here to help me, are you?"

"I am, but rather than help you I was going to suggest that we come to a mutual agreement that will benefit both our interests. You see I don't care if your family's deaths were accidents or if you intentionally killed them. It's irrelevant to me when I'm looking at the bigger picture."

"And what is the bigger picture?" Adam asked quietly.

"After Carla's call last night I put in a few calls of my own. Granting you asylum will, if it becomes known, cause a political shit storm. As you know relations between England and Scotland are tentative at best. As long as our Government denounces the actions of our militants and keeps up the pretence of cooperation then the relationship between the two nations is likely to remain the same. We do not have the military strength to effectively defend our country should this relationship deteriorate further and the English Government makes the decision to attack us. However, I very much doubt that they would want to start a war simply to retrieve a murderer, even one as high-profile as yourself. And based on what Carla told me about Ivan Williams I am doubtful that he want to keep you alive now."

Adam took a moment to comment on this. In the back of his mind he had suspected that Ivan might arrange for him to have an ‘accident’ whilst in custody, but hearing it from someone else made it harder somehow.

“So you’re going to help me?” he questioned after a short pause.

“As I said, the potential political fallout would cause my Government a headache, but we’ve decided that it is worth the trouble. For the right arrangement with yourself that is.”

“And what is the ‘right arrangement?’” Adam asked with interest. He had a feeling this was going to lead somewhere not quite unexpected, but perhaps further than he was prepared to go.

Jacobs smiled at the slight discomfort that Adam imagined he was displaying. “The Government would like to offer you a position as Head of their Technology Department. As you know Scotland is far behind England in terms of computing and military defence. In return for asylum we ask that you help us to catch up.”

“You said position,” Adam pointed out. “That implies that I’m not going to be working for free.”

“No. You will receive a wage plus bonuses for assisting with current projects that have stalled due to the inadequacy of current technical expertise.”

Adam almost laughed at this. “You believe that the technology here is one of the greatest evils yet you want my help to advance Scotland along the same lines?”

Jacobs wasn’t even fazed by Adam’s scepticism or tone. In fact he seemed delighted by it. “I knew I was right about you.”

“Really? What do you mean by that?”

“What was your first impression of me? Before Carla had told you the truth. What did you think of me?”

“Career boy,” Adam answered without hesitation. “Keen

to advance in Government by sticking to the rules and ass-kissing anyone you had to along the way."

Jacobs chuckled and shook his head. "Do you want to know what I thought of you?"

"I'm mildly intrigued."

"A troubled young man with great potential."

"Great potential?" Adam echoed with some disappointment. "Don't you know what Larimore Systems achieved because of me? I made millions for that company."

Jacobs shook his head. "Creating programs and building computer systems for commercial or Government use is a waste of that potential."

Adam did not reply to this and waited for Jacobs to continue. This wasn't how he had anticipated the conversation to play out at all and he'd be lying if he said he wasn't somewhat concerned by it.

"You would have been wasted at Larimore Systems. There is much more to you than your computer programming skills. You have the ability to change everything."

"Everything?" Adam repeated as he began to realise the real reason that Jacobs was here; not to just offer Adam asylum. "You don't just want me to help Scotland catch up do you?"

The older man smiled. "What I told Carla was true."

"But you didn't tell her everything about why you're really here and what you want my help for."

"Cards on the table," Jacobs replied without hesitation. "Scotland will grant you asylum, which I am hopeful we can keep secret from the English Government and L.S.A, and a job advancing our computer systems and defence programs. Our Government can also offer you something else you want, something I know you haven't let on to Carla."

"What's that?" Adam asked with intrigue.

"Revenge," Jacobs replied.

Adam laughed shortly. "Why would you guarantee me that?"

"Because we both want the same thing; the L.S.A destroyed and the fall of the English Government."

Adam tensed, immediately becoming guarded. "I just want Ivan to pay for what he did to me."

"And what greater pain for him than to see the destruction of everything that he has worked for."

Adam took a moment or two before replying. This wasn't what he had envisioned at all. He just wanted to make Ivan suffer.

"I'm not going to help you to take over the country," he said quietly.

"Scotland doesn't want to take over England; we want to save it. Since the Great Tsunamis England has fallen into a dictatorship. I'm sure you know your history. Before the disaster and war the people were given a free vote and a real say in the future of their nation. The retained title of Prime Minister is a mockery of this. In Scotland we have free elections and give the people a choice. I want to make a real difference here and change things for the better. Working with the current Government will not achieve this. Roberts had made his position on any proposed repeals of the genetics programme, for example, very clear and I doubt that things will improve once Sherrin takes over from him. Someone needs to make a stand for the people."

His words did strike a chord inside of Adam. He recalled those moments after his father's funeral. He had wanted to use

Larimore Systems to help people. That desire hadn't completely gone away, but it was buried underneath all the anger and hatred that he was feeling. Adam knew he couldn't shake this. He didn't want to. If he did then he was afraid that he would break down. He had to remain strong and focused on revenge.

Adam studied Jacobs as he mulled over the older man's words. He was talking like a leader not a follower, and in that moment Adam realised that he still wasn't being honest with him.

"Who are you really?" he demanded as he felt himself tense further. "You're not just a Scottish agent are you?"

"Adam—"

"Tell me the truth or you can forget everything. I'll find a way to get my revenge without your help."

"You're hardly in a position to be making any demands," Jacobs pointed out, however, his tone seemed more concerned than threatening.

Adam shrugged. "Maybe not but I don't have anything else to lose and you seem to need me."

Jacobs was silent for a minute before finally responding. "If I tell you then you will have to accompany my agents to Scotland. There will be no choice in this matter and should you refuse then you will be killed."

Some of Adam's confidence wavered at these serious words. Just what the hell was he about to get himself involved in? His hesitation only lasted a moment. Adam needed to leave London and he couldn't do that alone. Jacobs' offer was the only way. This didn't mean that Adam was going to allow himself to be used again.

"Tell me," he replied steadily. "Who are you?"

"I am the Head of the Scottish Intelligence Department."

Adam shook his head incredulously. "You expect me to believe that?"

"It is the truth."

"And the Government just allows you to moonlight as the Head of the Health and Lifestyle department in England?" Adam scoffed doubtfully. In truth Adam didn't know what to make of this. It sounded farfetched, but why would Jacobs lie to him?

"Do you have any proof?" Adam added.

"I can't carry I.D," Jacobs pointed out with mild amusement that cut through the tension between them. "You don't have to believe or trust me, but my offer still stands. I will grant you asylum and a chance for revenge. In exchange for the latter I need you to do something that will benefit our cause."

"What do you want me to do?"

"That will be explained once we are ready to make our move. Do we have an understanding, Adam?"

Again Adam lapsed into silence as he thought over Jacobs' proposal. So many people had lied to him and he didn't expect Jacobs to be any different. However, they both seemed to need each other's help. Adam couldn't bring himself to worry about what Jacobs had planned. As long as it hurt Ivan; that was all that he cared about. But what of the future? Did Jacobs expect that they might work together once their agreement had ended? Adam knew that he had no future and he needed to make sure that Jacobs understood this.

"You know I don't expect to live through this," Adam said quietly.

"I know," there was a tone of almost regret in Jacobs'

voice.

“Then we have an understanding.”

“Good,” Jacobs smiled.

CHAPTER EIGHTEEN

Jacobs left an hour later. He was due to leave the city and travel north on English Government business. For this he had a private aircraft that would take off from the roof of the Government's Health and Lifestyle offices in Sector Four. He told Adam that he needed to be at the building by 9pm and that he had arranged for two of his agents to escort Adam there.

Despite Adam's previous reservations the situation was playing out far better than he could ever have hoped.

It was 8.20pm now. Jacobs had said that he would speak to Carla and inform her that Adam was leaving. She hadn't arrived home yet. Adam hoped she would make it before he had to go. He wanted to thank her as well as say goodbye.

Adam had put on his old clothes that Carla had laundered and left the clothes that she'd given him. There was only one other thing Adam wanted to do before he left. He sat down on the sofa, switched on his computer and opened his camera application. Adam pressed 'record' and began to speak.

"Hi Ivan, as you're watching this I'll have left the city. You can waste countless man hours looking for me if you want, but I'm going somewhere that's out of even the L.S.A's jurisdiction. Congratulations on your promotion by the way. I hope it's everything that you wanted. Really. I do mean that. After all you betrayed me – and also your friendship with my father – to get it. So I hope it's worth all that at least. But don't get too comfy because it won't last. I'm going to make you pay for what you did to me. I'm going to take everything you care about and destroy it. As you and I both know, what happened to Joseph and Eleanor was an accident. I might have been a lot of things, but I wasn't a killer. Now things are very different. I will do whatever it takes to bring you down. I no longer have anything else to live for. Ruining your life is all I care about. And I will. You want a cold blooded killer. Fine, you'll get one. I wasn't a bad person, Ivan, I just needed your help. I hope you remember that when I take everything from you. You've brought this all on yourself."

Adam stopped recording. He attached the file to an email and set a timed delivery for 2am. By that time he would be well on his way to Scotland. Adam was under no illusions of what would happen now if Ivan caught him. He would have Adam killed. There was only one way that this would end. One of them would die. Dying didn't bother Adam. Why would it? He had nothing else to live for. He thought briefly of Leon and what might have been, but Leon had made his feelings perfectly clear and his lack of response to Adam's message had said it all. He was another person who had felt he could use Adam and then toss him aside. Adam was never going to let anyone use him like that again.

The sound of the door unlocking drew Adam from his

thoughts.

"Hi Carla," Adam greeted her as she hurriedly stepped over the threshold. "I'm just leaving a farewell message for Ivan," he smirked as he pressed the 'standby' button in the corner of the screen. "Don't worry he won't receive it until I'm long gone."

"Adam, we need to go. Now." Carla responded with clear agitation in her voice.

"Why? What's happened?"

"Dale called me. He said there's a patrol team heading this way to do a routine search of the building. They'll arrive shortly."

"Can't he call them off?"

"Not without it looking suspicious. We have some time, but we need to leave now."

"How much time?"

"A few minutes. Dale said we need to walk to the next block. He's told his agents to pick us up from there."

"Why can't they just pull up outside?"

"He's worried about them becoming compromised if you're seen. It could jeopardise his entire operation here."

Adam could see the reasoning behind this although a part of him was annoyed. After all he'd made an agreement with Jacobs. Quickly he grabbed his computer and put it into his bag before following Carla to the door.

"Here," Carla handed him a grey jacket. "Tuck your hair underneath and pull the hood up," she advised. "I'll check that the coast is clear."

"You don't have to come with me," Adam told her once she had returned and confirmed that it was.

"I want to," Carla insisted quietly. "Come on whilst it's

deserted."

Adam stepped ahead of her as they made their way into the hallway.

"Wait!" she hissed as she reached out to grab his arm. Adam quickly shrugged her off.

"If we look nervous it'll draw more attention," he pointed out. Carla didn't seem happy although she did not argue further. Adam led the way down the corridor. Thankfully at this time of night it was deserted.

Even though there was a lift between floors they opted to take the stairs. There was no one about and they made it outside without encountering a single person. On the streets it was different and Adam had already spotted several people on their way to or from work. Warehouse shifts went on all night so seeing people at different hours was common place. Casually Adam slung an arm around Carla's shoulders as they started to walk at a seemingly leisurely pace. If anyone got a good look at them they would realise who he was, but giving the impression that they were a couple wouldn't draw as much attention to them to begin with. After all, people would be looking for Adam on his own. The last thing they would expect was that he would have help from anyone. Carla played along and slipped an arm around his waist.

They both saw the two man patrol unit turning the corner and onto the street. Even though the officers were talking to each other they were alert and clearly keeping an eye on their surroundings. Adam and Carla discreetly changed direction, but this was picked up and they soon heard one of the officers calling out for them to stop.

"What do we do?" Carla asked softly, some panic entering her voice as the two sets of footsteps behind them broke into a jog.

Adam didn't know. If they ran then they would probably be shot at and Carla couldn't heal. It was too late anyway. A moment of indecision had cost them and the officers had now reached them. The first, a burly man in his fifties, shone a torch directly in Adam's face whilst his free hand yanked his hood down.

"That's him?" the other man, a younger guy in his mid-twenties, asked somewhat uncertainly.

"Yeah," the older officer confirmed. "Both of you turn around and put your hands on the wall," he commanded sternly. Carla was shaking as she did as they were told. Adam just stood there. He had seen the car that had just turned the corner and onto their street.

The older officer frowned in annoyance at Adam's failure to comply and roughly grabbed him by the shoulders. The man turned Adam around and shoved him against the steelwork. He felt the cold of the building against his cheek as the older officer conducted a swift search of him. The officer took Adam's bag containing his computer and set it down on the pavement beside him.

"Do not move," he told Adam sternly before he started to speak into his radio. "This is Officer Stephens. I have in my custody Adam Larimore and an unidentified—" he abruptly cut off and there was a thud that sounded like a body hitting the pavement. Moments later there was another. Only then did Adam turn around. Both of the officers were dead. Blood leaked steadily onto the cement from two neat bullet holes in the backs of their heads. Carla groaned and turned away. Even though she had probably seen much worse in the hospital Adam knew it was different witnessing the violence first hand.

Images of the lifeless bodies of his stepfamily once again came to the forefront of his mind and Adam had to struggle to force them aside when faced with this fresh slaughter.

The car door opened and two men dressed in identical charcoal business suits got out. The men hurried towards them. The older man with grey hair took hold of Adam's arm and began ushering him down the pavement and away from the bodies. Carla tried to go after him, but the second man blocked her path and tried to steer her back in the direction of the apartment block.

"Mr Larimore," the man holding onto Adam's arm spoke gruffly. His grip was tight enough that Adam couldn't break free of it. "We need to go."

"What about Carla?" Adam demanded as he made a token struggle against the man's hold on him.

"My colleague will ensure that she gets home, but we need to leave before another patrol unit arrives."

Without waiting for Adam's reply, the older man started to pull him in the direction of the car. Adam cast a glance over his shoulder and saw that Carla was being led back inside the apartment block. Adam was then practically forced into the back of the vehicle. The older man got into driver's seat. The car drew away from the pavement immediately and very quickly Carla and her apartment block were out of sight.

"I thought you were trying to be subtle?" Adam questioned in what he hoped was a casual voice in a bid to disguise the concern that he was feeling. Things had rapidly escalated and left him feeling as though he was no longer in control.

The older man frowned into the rear view mirror. "It would have been preferable," he acknowledged with some disapproval, "however, Mr Jacobs was very clear that we need to get you to Scotland no matter what."

"Did you have to kill them?" Adam asked quietly. In such a short space of time he had been exposed to so much death and he didn't think that it would end here.

"We can't leave any witnesses. You may be blamed for their deaths. That I'm afraid we cannot help."

Adam nodded. This didn't actually bother him as much as he thought it would. He would rather take the blame himself than Carla. Adam felt a pang of regret at the thought of his friend. He hadn't even been given a chance to say goodbye.

"Will you make sure that Carla's all right?" Adam requested worriedly. She had done so much for him and the last thing he wanted was her to be implicated in any way.

"Yeah," the older man confirmed. "Mr Jacobs will make sure of that."

Adam lapsed into silence as he watched the streets go by. So much had happened. So much that Adam still had some trouble coming to terms with it if he thought about it for too long. So he didn't. He remained focused on his anger and when the L.S.A headquarters flashed by as they continued on their way, Adam could only think of one day returning and exacting his revenge.

EPILOGUE

The Serpentines, Sector One, North London, 2115

Adam remained in his penthouse apartment for the rest of the day. He tried to busy himself with working on one of his programs, but he just couldn't get his conversation with Eric out of his mind.

As Adam knew he would Eric had eventually left. He was used to resolving conflicts and the hero just didn't know how to deal with Adam shutting him out like this. Adam was beginning to regret getting this involved with him. Eric didn't deserve this. He was more like Adam than perhaps he wanted to admit. They had both been lied to for most of their lives and they had both been used by the L.S.A and Ivan Williams for their own gains. Where they differed was how they wanted to go forward. Eric wanted to save London. Even after everything he had learned he still wanted to defend the city that he had been created to protect. There had been a time when Adam felt the same way. He had wanted to make a better life for the people who lived here, and in the rest of England, but he'd lost his way. He had become so focused on revenge that now nothing else mattered. And he still couldn't let it go. Not even for Eric.

Adam tensed when he heard the penthouse door sliding open.

"Mr Larimore?"

Carla. Adam felt himself relaxing again.

"Can I come in?" she asked hesitantly.

"Yeah," Adam replied. Out of all of his staff, Carla was the one whom he felt closest to. She had been his friend and ally from the beginning and without question or doubting him. Adam owed her so much more than saving his life.

"Are you all right?" she asked worriedly when she saw him sitting on the floor with his back against the side of the unmade bed. His portable computer was lying discarded beside him.

"Yeah."

"Have you taken your medication?" Carla enquired as she joined him on the floor.

The pills were still on Adam's bedside cabinet. Carla had prescribed them for his anxiety. They were also combined with a light sedative to help him sleep. Adam hadn't taken them since he arrived back at the Serpentines. He had hoped that he wouldn't need them anymore. He had been wrong and a day after he returned the familiar nightmares had surfaced again.

"Adam," Carla broke protocol and called him by his first name when Adam's lack of response told her all she needed to know. "You need to take them. You'll make yourself ill if you don't."

Adam knew she was right. Carla never prescribed medication unless it was absolutely necessary.

"I'm fine," he insisted regardless, but they both knew that wasn't true.

"Eric came to see me. He's really worried about you too."

Adam glanced up and recognised that expression of guilt on her face. Sometimes Carla hated the things that he asked her to do. But she would do them regardless. Her loyalty was to Adam and Dale Jacobs.

"What did he ask you?"

"He wanted to know what happened after you left London."

"And what did you tell him?"

"What we agreed," Carla almost snapped at him. "That I helped you to get to the border and that you were given asylum in Scotland."

"Thank you."

"Eric's a good guy and he doesn't deserve this. Have you thought about telling him the truth?"

Adam almost laughed at this. "He thinks I did."

"You still can. If you explain—"

"No," Adam cut her off. "It's too late now, Carla."

She sighed and shook her head. "He loves you, Mr Larimore. And I know you love him too."

Hearing it from someone else was painful. Adam got up and walked towards the window in a bid to disguise his upset. He wanted to deny it, but he couldn't bring himself to.

"Where is he now?" Adam asked instead.

"He's still in the cafeteria. I think—"

"I know you're trying to help, but please don't. I know what I'm doing."

"No," Carla shook her head. "You don't. You need to tell him."

Carla was only trying to help, but she really had no idea how far all this had gone.

"Please can you leave," he requested quietly.

"Okay," Carla replied. The disapproval and worry was clear in her voice. "Please do think about what I've said. It isn't too late."

Adam did not respond and without adding anything further Carla left him alone. Adam knew that Eric would come back later to talk to him. Even if Carla had put him off for now it wasn't in his nature to leave things unresolved like this. As much as Adam did want to tell him the truth, aside from it being too late he knew that if Eric learned the true path that he had set them on then he would never forgive Adam.

Adam closed his eyes as he recalled their almost meeting at the L.S.A party three years ago. It wasn't the first time he had thought of this or what might have happened had he been able to speak to Eric that night. Another regret. His life was full of them.

Adam cast those thoughts to the side and left his bedroom. He made his way over to his computer console and logged into the system. Eric would be arriving back here soon and Adam needed to convince him that his plan to expose the L.S.A was the best way for Eric to help him.

He doesn't deserve this

Adam winced as Carla's words echoed inside his head. She was right, Eric didn't deserve this. He deserved so much better. So had Adam.

I know you love him too

Adam did. More than anything, however, he had come

too far now. There was no turning back. Death and redemption came hand in hand with villainy and Adam wasn't naïve enough to think that he would be the exception. His life had ended three years ago when he had left London. Revenge was all that he had and after he'd achieved that…Adam smiled bitterly, painfully, to himself. That didn't matter. Nothing else mattered.

He heard the front door slide open. Adam didn't need to look up to know that it was Eric.

"What are you doing?" Adam cried out in utter disbelief as Ivan slammed his foot down on top of it. There was a crunch and the sound of metal breaking. Adam could hardly breathe. He stumbled back slightly, stunned and horrified at what he was witnessing. This couldn't be happening he told himself. Ivan was his godfather. He was supposed to look out for him.

"Climbing the career ladder," Ivan finally answered him. "I've often been criticised for my leniency where you're concerned. Being the arresting officer and charging you with two counts of murder will certainly discard any doubts Jeff Ingham has about my succession."

Adam forced away any lingering emotions as he recalled the still raw and painful memory of Ivan's betrayal.

You don't want this…not anymore

It didn't matter what he wanted, Adam thought with regret. He had learned this a long time ago.

ALSO BY SHARI SAKURAI

PERFECT WORLD
(PERFECT WORLD SERIES #1)

It is the year 2115 and the world is very different. With climate changes, natural disasters and war shaping the landscape, England has become a nation made up of several super cities and wasteland in between.

Eric Rawlins is a genetically engineered superhero created by the London Security Agency (L.S.A) to defend and protect the city against both national and international threats. With his superior abilities, celebrity status and beautiful girlfriend, Eric appears to have the perfect life. However, it is an illusion created by the L.S.A in order to control him.

Eric's nemesis is the charismatic Adam Larimore. The only son of billionaire business tycoon Victor Larimore, Adam is gifted with a genius level IQ as well as the same longevity as Eric.

When the actions of the L.S.A throw the two of them together Eric finds himself questioning everything that he has ever known as well as discovering the true course of events that led to Adam turning to a life of crime. As they become closer Eric realises that the L.S.A may be the real threat to London. But can he trust Adam or is he part of Adam's plan for revenge against those who have wronged him?

ABOUT THE AUTHOR

Shari Sakurai is a British author of paranormal, horror, science fiction and fantasy novels that almost always feature a LGBTQ protagonist and/or antagonist. She has always loved to write and it is her escape from the sometimes stressful modern life!

Aside from writing, Shari enjoys reading, watching movies, listening to (loud!) music, going to rock concerts and learning more about other societies and cultures. Japanese culture is of particular interest to her and she often incorporates Japanese themes and influences into her work.

Shari loves a challenge and has taken part and won the National Novel Writing Month challenge eleven times!

www.ingramcontent.com/pod-product-compliance
Lightning Source LLC
LaVergne TN
LVHW091129080826
845145LV00008B/2095
9780992802479